Like the generations of babas and nyonyas who traverse these stories, this book is a succulent mixture of colours, kebayas, *kerosang* and conversations, of scents, spicy food and feisty families. Lee Su Kim brings her sharp eye, her love of stories, and her keen sense of the verbal and visual to this delightful book which gives us a chance to savour the richness and diversity of Peranakan lives.

Professor Alastair Pennycook
University Technology Sydney, Australia

Mothers tell stories. Daughters often forget them but not Lee Su Kim. She shows that Malaysian Peranakan mothers transmit stories with a distinct flavour. Through these bright and trenchant vignettes, Su Kim has heightened the uniqueness of her community. One might add that these enjoyable tales also add a more nuanced dimension to the art of being both Malaysian and Chinese.

Professor Wang Gungwu
National University of Singapore, Singapore

A fascinating collection of tales bringing together the uniqueness of traditional Peranakan culture with universal human themes. By turns deeply moving and deliciously funny, these stories and the lives they portray go on reverberating in the mind long after reading them.

Professor Alan Maley, O.B.E.
Leeds Metropolitan University, UK

Kebaya Tales – each of its stories is evocative of different aspects of Peranakan heritage – is a sharing of cultural experience that will undoubtedly be an important part of Straits Chinese literature.

Dr Neil Khor
The Star, January 2011

If there were such a word as 'nyonyaness', this feminine book would epitomise that quality. These bitter-sweet stories have the diaphanous delicacy of an embroidered, lace-trimmed Swiss voile kebaya blouse, the dark richesse of the *buah keluak* – that Peranakan rival to the French truffle – combined with the piquant zest of a freshly pounded *sambal belacan*.

ILSA SHARP
Off The Edge, July 2011

Laced with gentle humour and candour, the stories cannot fail to draw the reader in ... Crafted around events and memories scandalous, momentous, heart-rending and even supernatural, the stories sparkle delightfully ... Su Kim also deftly captures moments that reflect our changing cultural mores, even down to delicate matters of the bedroom ... Pure reading pleasure from start to finish.

BABA EMERIC LAU
The Peranakan, 2011

Full-colour photographs [and] sepia prints from her family albums are creatively interspersed amongst the stories, with captions to explain the intricacies of the handiwork or the relationship to the author of the various family members. Coupled with *pantun* and popular ditties, the atmosphere of a bygone era comes alive in her book, the reverberations lingering till well after one puts the book down ... At times funny, whimsical and touching in parts, Su Kim writes fluidly, with an ear to the argot of her Nyonya heritage that manages to inform and hold the reader's attention.

SEE FOON CHAN-KOPPEN
Ipoh Echo, Dec 2011

Kebaya Tales

10th anniversary edition, with two new stories included

Of matriarchs, maidens, mistresses and matchmakers

Lee Su Kim

First published in 2011 by Marshall Cavendish (Malaysia) Sdn Bhd
This new edition published in 2020 by Marshall Cavendish Editions
An imprint of Marshall Cavendish International

Other Marshall Cavendish Offices:
Marshall Cavendish Corporation. 99 White Plains Road, Tarrytown NY 10591-9001, USA • Marshall Cavendish International (Thailand) Co Ltd. 253 Asoke, 12th Flr, Sukhumvit 21 Road, Klongtoey Nua, Wattana, Bangkok 10110, Thailand • Marshall Cavendish (Malaysia) Sdn Bhd, Times Subang, Lot 46, Subang Hi-Tech Industrial Park, Batu Tiga, 40000 Shah Alam, Selangor Darul Ehsan, Malaysia.

National Library Board, Singapore Cataloguing-in-Publication Data

Name(s): Lee, Su Kim.
Title: Kebaya tales : of matriarchs, maidens, mistresses and matchmakers / Lee Su Kim.
Description: New edition. | Singapore : Marshall Cavendish Editions, [2019] | "10th anniversary edition, with two new stories included"--Cover.
Identifier(s): OCN 1122928740 | ISBN 978-981-48-6875-4 (paperback)
Subject(s): LCSH: Peranakan (Asian people)--Fiction.
Classification: DDC M823--dc23

Printed in Singapore

Concept and layout of colour plates by Lee Su Kim. All kebayas and accessories featured are from the personal collection of the author. Photography by Lee Yu Kit and Lee Jan Ming. Photographs cannot be reproduced without the author's permission.

Dedicated to

STEPHEN J HALL

with love

And to the memory
of my parents,

LEE KOON LIANG &
FOO KWEE HOON

Contents

Preface to this Edition

When I first started writing *Kebaya Tales: Of Matriarchs, Maidens, Mistresses and Matchmakers*, I wondered how this book would be received. Who would be interested in reading stories about minority communities in a small country in South-east Asia? It is my pleasure to share that it has been an amazing and most satisfying 10-year writing journey. Six months after *Kebaya Tales* was published, the first print run was sold out. It has gone into several reprints since and is an award-winning bestseller today. It has been most warmly received and is sold not just regionally but in the UK, Europe, the US and Australia, and on many online portals. It is also used as a resource in language and literature courses in teacher's colleges and universities.

After *Kebaya Tales* was published in 2011, there was a clamour for more stories. With more stories in my head, and the fact that you can't have a kebaya without the accompanying sarong, I wrote my second collection, *Sarong Secrets: Of Love, Loss and Longing*, published three years later. In 2017, the trilogy was complete with a third collection, *Manek Mischiefs: Of Patriarchs, Playboys and Paramours*, named after the *kasut manek* (beaded slippers) and with the focus on the babas for a change. All three books were nominated for the national Popular-The Star Readers' Choice Awards (Fiction) with *Kebaya Tales* winning the first prize in 2011.

Where does your inspiration come from? I've often been asked this question. I am a sixth generation nyonya with links to both Malaccan and Penang Peranakan communities, as my father was a baba from Malacca and my mother a Penang nyonya. Coming from a unique and flamboyant culture with its share of eccentric personalities, complex cultural rituals, rich array of traditions and beliefs, a wonderful confluence of influences from Chinese, Malay, Indian, Javanese, Thai, Sumatran, Balinese, Portuguese, Dutch and English cultures, it's impossible not to be inspired. The sheer cultural hybridity of it all is absolutely fascinating. It struck me as strange there wasn't much fiction about the babas and nyonyas although there were many coffee table books and nonfiction.

I grew up in an extended family setting in a pre-war house in Jalan Sin Chew Kee, off Galloway Road, Kuala Lumpur. Relatives, friends and neighbours dropped by often, and I loved to listen to the chatter and stories. My mother, a superb storyteller, with her dramatic flourishes and onomatopoeia, was also a fantastic cook, attracting even more visitors because they loved her food. My family observed the traditional rituals, celebrated the festivals, honoured our ancestors, cooked fabulous feasts. Thus I grew up with an insider knowledge of the smells, sounds, flavours, noises, cadences and the belief systems of a traditional baba nyonya household. I was exposed from young to a multitude of languages: English, Baba Malay, Penang Hokkien, Cantonese, Hakka, Malay as well as idioms, earthy expressions, swear words and the fascinating *berlatah* (ranting) of the *bibiks* (older nyonyas). Attending auspicious occasions such as weddings and birthday celebrations and funerals and visiting relatives in Malacca, Penang and Singapore also gave me exposure to more cultural content, though I'd no clue then I would write about the babas and nyonyas one day.

My purpose in writing is to try and capture the spirit of this culture, its very essence – its cultural hybridity, colour and opulence, its eccentricities and idiosyncrasies, its openness to myriad cultures, its array of intriguing personalities – as well as its less attractive features – its patriarchal structures, rigid social mores, the lack of opportunity for women in the 19th to early 20th centuries.

Altogether, *Kebaya Tales*, *Sarong Secrets* and *Manek Mischiefs* contain a total of 35 short stories, spanning the 19th century to the present. One can discern from the stories how the community has evolved, the issues it faces, its challenges and silent identity struggles, its resilience, its beauty and imperfections. Stories are living expressions of our diverse cultures and shared memories. With increasing homogeneity through globalisation, it has become all the more important to keep our individual cultures alive as expressions of our rich cultural diversity. They capture the zeitgeist of the day. While the perspective of my stories is through the lens of the baba-nyonya, the themes are, really, at the end of the day, human universal themes.

Over the ten years since I wrote *Kebaya Tales*, I have observed a yearning amongst my readers to know more about our localised identities, a deep pride in and appreciation of our history and heritage. The stories also evoked memories amongst readers who had lost touch with their past. A number of young readers informed me that my stories reminded them of their grandmothers and their childhood, leading to a rekindling of ties and seeking of knowledge. One young girl thanked me at a talk I gave and said she didn't know she was a nyonya till she read *Kebaya Tales* and found that the cultural practices, food, language, idiomatic expressions and lifestyles in the stories were all prevalent in her growing-up years and that her grandmother wore the same clothes described in the book. Several readers living in the UK, Europe and US felt nostalgic and sought to touch base again with their 'lost' culture or with members of the larger international community. This sparking of journeys of identity and self-discovery was an unexpected and most rewarding outcome.

As for my own personal journey, it is heartening to see a continuing resurgence of interest in the Peranakan baba nyonya culture. When once it was predicted to go the way of the dodo bird, today it is still alive and evolving in various ways. The Internet has played a large part in connecting Peranakan communities all over the world, sharing and disseminating information. Of course there will always be reinterpretations and concerns about commodification and Disneyfication but that, I guess, is the price of a broadening appeal and interest in the culture.

Cultural activism in my roles as a founding member and the Founding President of the Peranakan Baba Nyonya Association of Kuala Lumpur and Selangor (PPBNKLS) from 2005 till 2014 and as a member of several Peranakan associations, heritage advocacy organisations and multiple Facebook groups, giving talks and readings at heritage and literary events, all helped me to connect with a vast network of Peranakans and heritage enthusiasts all over the world and stay tuned to the goings-on of the community. A TEDx talk I gave on my journey titled "A Nyonya Journey" in October 2017 for TEDx Petaling Street attracted 25,000 views on YouTube to date, reflecting keen and continuing interest.

It wasn't easy when I started writing *Kebaya Tales* ten years ago. It is hard enough trying to capture the nuances of a specific ethnic group while writing in English, what more when describing a complex hybrid community and a fusion culture. There was also a lack of precedents. How does one capture the sheer flamboyance and exuberance of this unique culture? Would I ever do justice to it? I hope I have, in a small way. In the process, I've enjoyed this journey very much – it has enriched me personally and I am grateful to all of you who have given me your encouragement, support and appreciation.

Kebaya Tales: Of Matriarchs, Maidens, Mistresses and *Matchmakers* now returns as a 10th anniversary edition with new stories. I thank my publisher, Marshall Cavendish International (Asia) and Leslie Lim from Pansing Distribution for their enthusiastic support in pushing for a new edition.

Kebaya Tales returns with two brand new short stories, both based on real events. *The Peephole* is not fictitious, but based on my own experience. Till today I am puzzled by the strange sighting. The other story, *Hitam Manis and the Majestic Mayfair Hair Salon*, will resonate with many readers who are familiar with identity politics and skin colour.

To my son, Jan Ming, who has been most helpful reading my new stories and giving enthusiastic feedback – I thank you for your interest and joyful support. To She-reen Wong, my editor, you are a pleasure to work with – I am ever grateful to you for your feedback, interest and efficiency. As always, thank you, Stephen Hall, for your abiding patience, encouragement and support. When I sometimes falter or procrastinate, it is your love and belief in me that keep me going. The journey has been all the richer and easier with you by my side.

Lee Su Kim
November 2019

Acknowledgements

I am indebted to my mother, Foo Kwee Hoon, an unforgettable nyonya – witty, feisty and funny when she wanted to be. She could spin a good story and hold her audience spellbound, especially my father, who loved her till the end of his days. To my aunt, Foo Kwee Sim, whose memories of those long-ago days are still as fresh as her *otak-otak*, thank you for sharing such delightful stories. I am grateful to my aunt, Lee Mey Ling, whose beauty sent many hearts aflutter on Chap Goh Meh, thank you for good times together and insights into the lives of the nyonyas.

I thank my uncles, both amazing storytellers, Babas Foo Yat Kee and Foo Yat Chin, for details of the Japanese Occupation and riveting stories. My thanks go to my sister, Su Win, for her kind assistance, and my friend, Harriet Wong, whose own story of the painting of an old shophouse in Malacca inspired me deeply. Thank you, Harriet, for always encouraging me to write. To Professors Alan Maley and Jayakaran Mukundan, thank you for your belief in my work and your keen interest. To Rocky Carruthers, for her assistance and enthusiastic support. To Aunty Kim, famous kebaya maker from Penang, I have enjoyed our wonderful conversations about kebayas. To Barbara Fras of the Peranakan Museum, Singapore, thank you for believing in this book. My thanks also go to Marshall Cavendish, to Christine Chong,

Irene Leow and Lee Mei Lin for their support.

I would like to thank the Presidents of the Peranakan Associations of Singapore, Malacca, Penang, Thailand and Australia (at the time of writing the first edition) – Peter Wee, Datuk Phua Jin Hock, Dato'Seri Khoo Keat Siew, Dr Kosol Tanguthai and Alfred Chi respectively – and Victor Goh, President of Gunung Sayang Association, for their friendship and support. My thanks go to Babas Lee Kip Lee, past President of the Peranakan Association of Singapore, Dr Neil Khor, Peter Lee, Chan Eng Thai and Pranee Sakulpipatana for their interest and kind advice, and to all my friends in the Peranakan Baba Nyonya Association of Kuala Lumpur & Selangor (PPBNKLS) and all the other Peranakan associations in the Asia-Pacific. To all my friends and readers, thank you for your support and constant encouragement to me to keep on writing.

I am truly indebted to my cousin, Lee Yu Kit, for his photographs – his creative expertise is much appreciated – and Siew Chi for her interest and encouragement.

I'd like to thank my son, Jan Ming, whose keen interest in these stories helped to spur me on. Thank you for all the lovely photos you took for me. Finally, to my husband Stephen Hall – it wouldn't have been possible without your love, friendship, advice and unfailing support. Thank you for your insightful comments and feedback, and for giving me the space and peace to write. Your deep interest in my Peranakan heritage continues to inspire me to carry on writing and exploring more facets of this unique culture.

About the Babas and Nyonyas

Origins

The babas and nyonyas of Malaysia and Singapore are a unique ethnic group which originated 700 years ago when Chinese traders arrived in Malacca, the centre of the Malacca Sultanate. The traders sojourned in Malacca for around six months, waiting for the monsoons to change direction and bring them home to Fujian, on China's southeastern coast. They did not bring their women folk along and many intermarried with the local women. It was from these crosscultural unions that the babas and nyonyas evolved. Intermarriage between the babas and the local women eventually ceased, and for hundreds of years past, the babas married exclusively amongst their own people, becoming an endogamous and elite group.

Another interesting theory as to the origins of the babas and nyonyas is the legend of the Chinese princess, Hang Li Po, sent to marry the Sultan of Malacca to boost diplomatic ties between Malacca and China. The *Malay Annals* describes vividly the arrival of the Chinese princess Hang Liu in Malacca with an entourage of five hundred ladies and courtiers. The princess and her retinue settled down at a place called Bukit China. The Sultan of Malacca, Sultan Mansur Shah, ordered a well dug at the foot of Bukit China for his Chinese bride. Both the well, Perigi Hang Li Po, and Bukit China are still in existence in Malacca today.

The babas and nyonyas are also known as the Peranakan, the Straits Chinese and Straits-born Chinese. The word 'Peranakan' is derived from the Malay word '*anak*' which means 'child'. The term refers to local-born as well as the offspring of foreigner-native union. Baba is an honorific from northern India for 'man', nyonya is an honorific for 'woman' in Malay adopted from the Portuguese word for grandmother.

Culture

The Baba nyonya culture is a rare and beautiful blend of many cultures – Chinese and Malay, mixed with elements from Javanese, Sumatran, Thai, Burmese, Balinese, Indian, Portuguese, Dutch and English cultures. The influence of European elements was because Malacca was conquered by three colonial powers successively: the Portuguese in 1511, the Dutch in 1641 and the British in 1824.

The culture is very much localised in essence, and proudly Chinese in form. The babas kept to their patriarchal culture, with male offsprings bearing the family name, while the mother culture was maintained by the womenfolk. In Malacca and Singapore, the Peranakan spoke Baba Malay, a patois of the Malay language with many loan words from Hokkien and English. In Penang, Hokkien was spoken instead of Baba Malay. The customs were heavily Chinese in form, as the babas and nyonyas clung loyally to their Chinese identity. Filial piety was very important and ancestral worship was core to the culture.

The lifestyle of the nyonyas was a unique balance between Chinese and Malay world traditions. The traditional nyonya costume was the *baju panjang* which can be traced to Javanese origins. It consisted of a long, loose calf-length top with long sleeves worn over a batik sarong. The collar is Chinese and the dress is fastened by a set of *kerosang* (three brooches linked by a gold chain).

By the end of the 1920s, young nyonyas abandoned the austere *baju panjang* for the more attractive nyonya kebaya. The short kebaya was more flattering and shapely, with intricate embroidery at the neckline, sleeves and hem. Nyonyas preferred the Pekalongan batik sarongs from Java because of their vibrant colours and motifs of birds, flowers and animals.

Nyonya food is a wonderful combination of Malay and Chinese cuisine with Southeast Asian and European influences. Using a variety of ingredients and cooking methods, herbs and spices and occasionally, western influences such as Worcester sauce, the nyonyas concocted a unique cuisine — the original fusion food with predominantly hot, spicy and piquant flavours. Peranakan cuisine is labour intensive and considered an art. Condiments are important on the nyonya's dining table especially the ubiquitous *sambal belachan*. A nyonya's cooking ability could be assessed, in the olden days, from the rhythms of the way she pounded the *sambal belachan*.

The babas and nyonyas today

Today, the baba and nyonya community still survives with its strongholds in Malacca, Penang and Singapore. Many younger generations of Peranakan have moved to live and work in Kuala Lumpur. (There are also Peranakan communities in Kelantan and Terengganu on the east coast of Peninsular Malaya; Phuket, Thailand; Indonesia, Myanmar, Laos and Vietnam.) With globalisation and further migration, the Peranakans have settled all over the world with large communities in Melbourne, Sydney and London.

Both the old historic Quarters of Georgetown and Malacca, where Peranakan enclaves are located with its unique architecture and lifestyles, were declared World Heritage Sites by UNESCO in 2009.

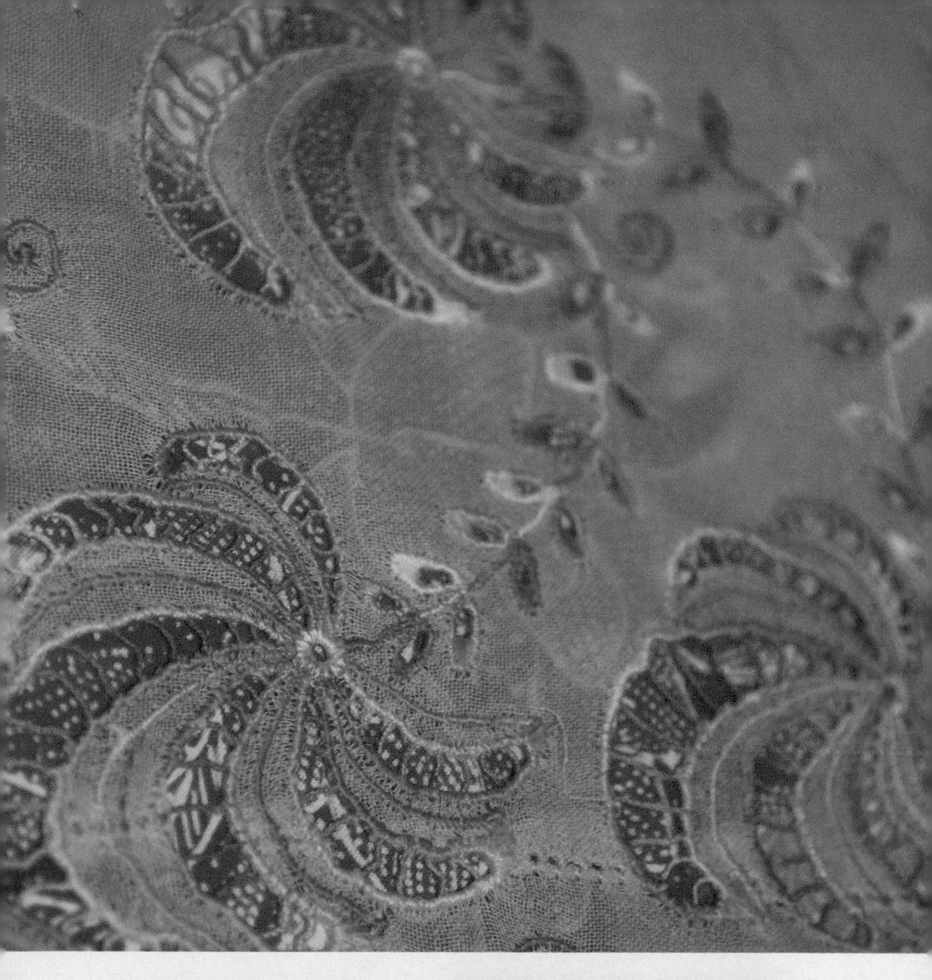

Kebayas are the beautifully embroidered blouses worn by the nyonyas and matched with sarongs. Its origin is obscure but is believed to have come from Java. The word 'kebaya' comes from the Portuguese word 'kobaya'. Wearing a kebaya is like reconnecting with another world – the world of the nyonyas which moves at a gentler, more languid pace.

Browsing through old kebayas, touching the light diaphanous material, I can't help but think of the nyonyas who used to wear them. Who were they? What were their lives like? What is the significance of the embroidery or the colours chosen? What are the stories hidden in the soft folds and delicate lace of these beautiful kebayas?

Hitam Manis and the Majestic Mayfair Hair Salon

Rachel gritted her teeth and braced herself as they arrived at the entrance of the Majestic Mayfair Hair Salon on Bukit Bintang Road. She knew she'd be subjected to it again – the cluckety-clucks, the tsk-tsks of disapproval, the stares of horror from the lady boss and her coterie of lily-white shampoo girls. There was simply no escape.

She had just returned from a camping trip with her friends – seven days of swimming, snorkeling and sunbathing, not that she needed to sunbathe as she tanned naturally very quickly in the sun. She now sported an even more gorgeous tan – a lustrous dark brown, the colour of gula melaka. Her camping mates, Maisie and Ley Ley, had merely turned red as lobsters whilst Foong Wan had ended up with painful sunburn. Not Rachel.

Her father's nickname for her was Hitam Manis (black and sweet). It was her Pa who taught her to take pride in her colouring, assuring her it was perfectly okay. Although she was Chinese, she didn't have to be fair-skinned like the rest of her Chinese schoolmates, he pointed out. After all, she was a tenth generation nyonya and the babas and nyonyas, from the beginning, came in all shades and colours, from *putih* (white) to honey golden to caramel and milk-coffee tones.

Mr Lee, Rachel's father, found that his daughter took like a duck to water at a very young age. She was a natural, fearless even after she toppled into the enormous urn of rainwater in the kitchen courtyard and was fished out in time thanks to the hysterical barks of Macky, the pet beagle. During the school holidays, her father took the family on holiday trips to the company seaside chalet at the Blue Lagoon and taught her to swim and float in the sea.

When she reached her teens, he drove her, after work, to the Weld swimming pool every Tuesday and Thursday. He hired Encik Othman, a private coach, to give her swimming lessons. By the time she was fourteen, she had become an excellent swimmer and represented her school in competitive swimming. At sixteen, she won two gold medals in the National Swimming Championships for the 100 meters and 200 meters breaststroke events. With the hours of training in the pool, holidays by the sea and her natural dusky complexion, Rachel was always the brownest Chinese girl in her school.

This wasn't a problem at all. It only became a problem when she accompanied her mother to the Majestic Mayfair Hair Salon, her mother's favourite hair salon. It was run by a short, attractive but rather crass woman with bleached blondish hair by the name of Delilah Faustina Pong, a name she gave herself as she abhorred her real name, Pong Ah Moi. She spoke excellent Cantonese and Mandarin and believed she spoke very good English too.

Madam Delilah's outstanding feature was her fair, white skin that had never been touched by the sun by the looks of it. The salon customers praised her fairness to no end, which made her glow even more with pride. Although pregnant at the time, she had taken to wearing miniskirts to show off her stark white legs. Proud of her snow-white complexion, she worked hard to keep it pristine, slathering whitening creams and moisturisers frequently, gazing askance at any mirror available, which wasn't difficult as her entire salon was lined with wall mirrors.

She loathed having anything to do with nature. Whenever she had to step out, she'd groan, "Aiyaah, chan hai CHUNG sei sai yitt tow!" (I HATE getting burnt by the sun!), even if it was just to get something from her car parked outside. After work at 6 pm, she'd don long gloves to protect her hands and arms, and a huge straw hat, and dash to her car, clutching a gargantuan golf umbrella over her. She was a tough businesswoman, capable and hardworking, in her salon seven days a week, bossing and ordering her workers around. Highly opinionated, she firmly believed that fairness – even better, whiteness – was the ultimate standard for beauty, especially if you were Chinese.

"I can't bear that loud Delilah woman and her patronising remarks," grumbled Rachel to her mother. "Mum, do we have to go today? She's bound to say something nasty to me."

She didn't want to step into the salon after her recent sun-soaked island trip but her mother had decided at the last minute to drop in for a quick hair trim before their shopping jaunt.

Rachel's mother tried to rationalise. "She's just like that – totally tactless. She doesn't mean to insult you. Everything is either black or white with her. There's no gray area."

"Well, in her case it's definitely only white!" Rachel complained.

"Just ignore her," Rachel's mother advised, "and for goodness sake, don't answer back as it reflects badly on me."

Rachel stepped into the salon, wishing she'd worn long sleeves instead of a sleeveless top. Of all days, why did she choose the yellow halter neck that would show up her tan even more?

The Majestic Mayfair Hair Salon didn't quite live up to its majestic name. The overpowering perm chemicals assaulted your senses when you walked in, the floor was littered with unswept hair, scraggly outworn towels draped over a rickety towel rack under a high-speed, whirling ceiling fan. Boxes of perm and shampoo products lay scattered about and the counters were cluttered with magazines, scissors, combs, curlers and hairdryers. The dark green paint on the walls was peeling off at the edges, wires criss-crossed the floor haphazardly. Madam Delilah didn't seem to have a proper system in place. However, she was always fashionably dressed, with glossy pink lipstick, rouged cheeks, darkened eyebrows, heavy mascara, her permed hair coifed in the latest hairstyles.

Her business was thriving as it was the only hair salon in the neighbourhood, her rates were quite reasonable, and best of all, one could catch up on all the gossip. Did Uncle Tong walk out on his one-kind-of-fierce, husband-beating wife? What about Latifa – anyone knows if she ran off to Thailand to marry her already-married Datuk boyfriend? And that Mrs Chan – did she win 500 ringgit or 50,000 ringgit in the Empat Nombor Ekor Lucky Draw? She hasn't been forthcoming in her answer! And did Suriyati, Mrs Leong's maid, steal the missing US dollars from the study room or was it her own Alzheimer-ish mother who went missing herself two days ago? And wahhh, why is the price of *kangkung* going up nowadays?

Madam Delilah greeted Rachel's mum sweetly, oozing smiles and charm, as Mrs Lee and her daughter walked in. Her PR skills were exceptional especially when there was money to be made.

"*Chow sun*. Gud morning, Mrs Lee, *nei how mah?* Sit down, sit down, anywhere oso can, ahhh, here gud, got aircon."

"Chinese tea or coffee? Plain water also got. What you want? I get for you, no poblum."

She fussed over Rachel's mum while Rachel quickly slipped onto the nearest available chair and buried her head in a magazine with a Hong Kong starlet pouting prettily on its cover.

"Mrs Lee ah, wahh, your silver hair so bootiful, so shining, I oso wan hor," she exclaimed, touching Mrs Lee's greying salt and pepper hair gingerly.

Then, she noticed Rachel sitting in the next chair and shrieked, "Aiyah! *Chow meh sai tow kam hak kah?* Larstime you oredi chocolate colour but this time ah, you *sudah hangus* ... how you say ah ... you burnt oredi!"

Rachel's head emerged from the huge glossy magazine with an ugly scowl then submerged again.

"See, Mum, I told you so. I knew she'd comment! What more, in tongues!" Rachel retorted in a muffled tone, head buried between pages 22 and 23 featuring glamorous Hong Kong and Taiwanese actresses in flamboyant gowns and exquisite *chi paos*, Photoshopped to a dazzling white.

The other shampoo girls, Ah Lan and Ah Chan, busy at work shampooing customers' heads, turned around to stare at Rachel and frowned in disapproval.

Only Mei Mei the youngest shampoo girl, less pallid in complexion, was more sympathetic. "Okay what. Very healthy-looking."

Madam Delilah stood stupefied and gawked in horror at Rachel's reflection in the mirror.

"Aiyahh, Mrs Lee ah," she admonished Rachel's mother, "why you let your daughter become like that one ... die lor, next time who want to marry her?"

This irritated Rachel to no end. She was in the throes of first love with the captain of the Selangor swimming and waterpolo team, a super-toned, super-tanned, good-looking sixth former named Joon Leong. When he took off his tracksuit top to reveal his muscled torso, broad shoulders and slim hips, the girls in the swimming team went into a tizzy. He was a strong, powerful swimmer – his front crawl was superbly graceful and effortless, his hands slicing the surface of the water in neat crisp strokes, his mighty kicks propelling him forward as if charged by an underwater turbo engine, leaving the competition floundering behind. He had a personality to match – warm, caring, intelligent and kind. Although immensely popular and quite the star athlete, he was unassuming with a charming, self-deprecatory sense of humour. She was blissfully besotted.

Rachel found her feelings for him were not unrequited. He seemed to be attracted to her too, cheering himself hoarse for her when she competed in the breaststroke events, buying her drinks and ice kacang at the canteen, helping her to carry her towel and bags, always by her side amidst the triumphs, struggles, tears and exhilaration in the world of competitive swimming.

Rachel slammed the magazine down on the counter, sending combs and curlers flying, and snapped, "Oi, you all know or not? In America, they will pay a fortune to have my tan!"

Mrs Lee was relieved at her daughter's response. Going head on with Madame Delilah Pong was pointless.

"I donch believe! Talk nonsense. How much?" Madam Delilah asked skeptically.

Ah Chan chimed in, "Boss, you open a salon there!"

"It's true. In the West, they love to look tanned, it means you've got money to fly to the tropics for a holiday. A tan is a status symbol there," said someone who couldn't be recognised as her long thick tresses were swept down over her face for a colouring job.

"I thoth ith becuth ofth winter. Inth winter everyth bodyth turn whiteth and paleth," offered Miss Liew, hairpins in mouth, trying to help Ah Chan roll her rigidly-straight hair in curlers.

To Rachel's relief, that diverted the topic of conversation from her dire lack of prospects in the marriage market to the crazy, filthy-rich Americans and mad *kwei lo* who spent all their holidays roasting in the crazy hot sun.

Five months later, news got around from patrons of the Majestic Mayfair Hair Salon that the lady boss had given birth to a pair of twin girls and both mother and twins were doing well.

Rachel dropped in at the salon one Saturday morning as she badly needed a haircut – her hair was getting dry with split ends due to too much sun and chlorine. She hoped fervently Madame Delilah would still be on maternity leave. She wasn't in the mood for any stupid comments.

Madam Delilah decided to turn up at her salon that very same day, bringing her twins along for the first time. She honked loudly from her car parked outside to announce her arrival. Ah Lan automatically grabbed the nearest umbrella and dashed outside. Delilah sauntered in eventually, dressed in slinky fuchsia, wheeling in a large pram with the twins inside in matching pink, with Ah Lan holding a mammoth yellow umbrella decorously above them as if escorting royalty.

The customers crowded around the pram to look at the twins. They were adorable, dressed in pinafores with white caps and white baby gloves, feet in lace-trimmed socks and the cutest baby shoes. They smiled and chuckled, looking around in wide-eyed wonder at the faces hovering above, cooing, dribbling in baby talk. The two girls looked exactly alike and resembled their mother, everyone agreed.

But there was something odd. Very odd indeed. Everyone stared but no one dared to comment. Nobody said anything until Puan Latifa, now Wife Number Two but without the Datin title, blabbed, "Eh-eh, *macam mana ni?* What happened? How come one *kopi susu* and one *susu?* One brown like café latte and one white like milk?"

Madam Pong glowered. "I donch know."

"Never mind, at least you won't have any problems trying to figure out which twin is which," said Mrs Pathma helpfully.

"Ei, any more smart comments? Tink you all very clever, izzit?! Can give birth to two or not – at one go?!" challenged Madame Delilah. She scowled and looked as if she'd happily strangle the next person who dared say one more word.

After barking instructions to her workers and checking the accounts, Madame Delilah announced she and the twins had to leave for the pediatrician's.

Rachel managed to say, "Congratulations, Aunty Delilah" and got a killer glare from her instead. She stormed out with the twins who were fretting and crying by now, accompanied by poor Ah Lan wielding two umbrellas this time, one to shade her boss and the other the twins.

After Madame Delilah had driven away, Ah Lan scurried back into the salon and gleefully announced, "Now Boss gone, I tell you all something ah ... but you all don't tell her I told you. Like this ah ... after the twins were born, big fight between my boss and her *low koong* ... er ... I mean her husband. Mr Pong asked Mrs Pong, 'Eh, why the twins come in two colours hah? One white, one chocolate. What you doing behind my back?' Mrs Pong gave him one tight slap and said, 'You *theeen low* ... you mad man ... I so busy everyday working like *theeen por* ... mad woman ...you think I got time to have affair meh!'

"You know lah, my Bossy very fierce so Mr Pong give up and went back to his kampong in Kampar because his 90-year-old father died, nobody left. He go back to his old house to do spring cleaning, he throw, throw, throw out a lot of things. Then ..."

Ah Lan paused dramatically.

She relished the sight of all the customers wrapped in plastic sheets, towels around their necks, in various stages of haircuts, shampoo washes and perms, hanging to her every word.

"Then what?"

"Then who?"

"Then how?"

"Then Mr Pong got a shock. He found a pile of very old photos and saw a scary-looking old grandmother in a sarong and *baju panjang*. Somemore ah, she look like him, especially the high forehead. He drove, drove, drove all the way to Alor Gajah to ask his aunty, his father's sister, 92 years old but eyesight still okay, who is this woman in the photo?"

Ah Lan paused again when Mrs Thin, head stuck inside the steaming machine emitting voluminous clouds of steam, protested loudly, "*Fai-tik lah*! Faster, faster tell! Always stopping for what?!"

Ah Lan hastily continued, "Mr Pong's aunty said, 'Hah? You don't know? You don't know this person in the photo? She is your father's grandmother. Your great-grandmother! Your father never told you about her? Aiyahh, that's the problem, you busy young people never bother to ask.' Mr Pong ask, 'Why she dress like that, no trousers?' Old aunty told him, 'Your great grandmother was a nyonya from Sumatra. Very rich family in Medan. Very fierce woman, always chewing *sireh* and spitting out red colour spit. Her name was Putih but she changed her name to Hitam because she was very dark and she hate white colour because she say look like *hantu* ... er ... *kwei* ... er ... I mean, ghost.' "

Ah Lan concluded with an ear-to-ear grin, "Hahaha. So funny hor."

She gave a little bow then returned to her task of scratching her customer's scalp smothered in foamy bubbles with her long fingernails. Rachel and everyone else were utterly gobsmacked and forgot to clap.

After her haircut by Mei Mei, the resident stylist in her boss's absence, Rachel walked out of the Majestic Mayfair Hair Salon trying hard to smother an onslaught of hysterical giggles.

Joon Leong was outside waiting for her. His face lit up when he caught sight of her. He murmured disarmingly, "Hello, Butterscotch babe."

She smiled and took his bronzed, outstretched hand. Together they walked hand in hand to the Weld swimming pool for swimming practice.

The Peephole

Grandpa had bought the old prewar house for a mere 7,000 ringgit in 1931. It was located in a quiet residential area tucked away right in the heart of Kuala Lumpur. Although not as heavily stylised or ornamented as the terrace houses along Hereen Street, Malacca, it had similar interesting features such as Grecian columns, spacious verandahs, prohibitively high ceilings and an inner open courtyard. Grandma, with her love for flamboyant colours, re-tiled the plain floor with Italian tiles in starburst patterns of rustic brown, orange and indigo.

Stepping into the house felt like stepping into an adventure. The house seemed to go on and on, its short façade compensated by its length. There were two halls: the front hall where guests sat and chatted, drank cold coffee brewed early in the morning from a big, fat stainless steel pot, and behind an ornate divider, the second hall, which served as a "free-for-all" – study room/sewing room/TV room/dressing room and siesta room. On one side was a steep wooden staircase tilted at a formidable 45-degree angle bordered by an elegant carved bannister. Another attractive feature was the open courtyard or "airwell" where Mother dried her spices on wicker trays and colourful sarongs on bamboo poles. Raindrops splattered in and soft breezes blew into this space, cooling the house. At night we could see the moon peeping behind darkish clouds or the stars twinkling above us.

However, it was the peephole on the floor of the huge bedroom upstairs that I loved the most. With no doorbell in those days in the 1960s, visitors had to come right up to the verandah and knock on the front door. All one had to do was look through the peephole overlooking the verandah to see who it was. None of the eighteen houses along that street had this feature. Grandma probably added it along with the Italian tiles.

As a child, prankish and precocious, I enjoyed tossing little toys and confetti – bits of paper torn out of old newspapers – down that peephole on visitors who came a-calling. My little brother and I would clamber like crazed monkeys up the narrow twenty-two steps and run to the peephole to check. The puzzled visitor, on looking up, would see a square-cut hole about three inches wide right above him, occupied by a human eye. Sporting uncles who dropped by to visit would smile and holler, "Hey, just you wait! I'll get you, little rascals!" and not-so-sporting, vain aunties would screech, "Oi, nothing better to do ah? You're ruining my hairdo. *Celakak!*" My brother and I would squeal and jump up and down with delight, then run off to hide behind the many doors of that wonderful old house or in its myriad nooks and corners.

Sometimes when irritating salesmen, overzealous preachers or dubious donation seekers refused to leave, we'd spit on them through the peephole. They would storm off in disgust and never bothered us again, much to my parents' puzzlement, unaware of our shenanigans above.

I was the self-appointed Keeper of the Peephole. My bed was nearest to it so whenever I heard noises or voices below, I'd be the first to scramble to survey the scene. The tops of heads were always what I usually saw: beautifully coiffured heads, permed hair heads, straight jet-black hair heads, greying hair heads, pony-tailed heads, short cropped heads, *botak* (bald) heads, crewcut heads, diamante hairpins in buns heads, beehived-styled heads, jasmine in *sanggul*-ed heads.

I had to figure out who they might belong to. It was a difficult angle to make out the person really. If I couldn't, I'd growl an omnipotent, scary "Hellooo. Who are yoouuu?" through the peephole. On other days, I'd impetuously demand an answer, "Password? Password or you die ..." The unsuspecting visitor would look around, startled, and then up in alarm, and I'd be able to report who I thought it was.

I slept upstairs in the front room with my siblings and Grandma. My parents occupied the last room at the back while Grandpa slept in the middle room all by himself. His snoring was so loud no one wanted to sleep with him, including Grandma. She was married off to Grandpa at the very early age of 16 in an arranged marriage. She was only 10 when she was pulled out of school because her parents were concerned she would become too educated, too *bebas* (independent). She resented the premature termination of her education and reminded me often how lucky I was to be born at the right time. She was convinced that had she been born in my era, she would have become a very successful lawyer or doctor.

While many arranged marriages worked out well in those days and love came after marriage, it wasn't the case with Grandma. I always had the feeling she merely put up with Grandpa. She disliked Grandpa's laidback ways and his lack of ambition. He had retired very early from a government job because of a stroke and loved to boast to anyone who would listen that his monthly pensions far outnumbered his salaries. They only talked when necessary and while they didn't have any massive quarrels, they didn't engage in much conversation either and led their own separate lives.

I was only ten years old when something strange happened via that peephole. I've given up telling anyone about it: When you reach your golden years and you talk about events from your childhood, people think you're entering it again.

We had just had supper that night. Lots of itinerant hawkers and peddlers came around to our street in those days. The Rojak man, the Ice Cream man, the Yong Tow Foo man, the Fishball Soup man, the Candy man, the Satay man, the Tong Sui man, the Roast Duck man – all throughout the day, there would be a parade of hawkers calling out their wares and signalling their arrival with songs, shouts, bells, horns and whistles.

Ah Soon, the Dim Sum man, came by around ten at night. Folks slept early in those days and the street was usually quiet and still except for the singing of the unseen cicada orchestra. At the sound of the roaring carbide lamp and the signature tune of Ah Soon – "*siew mai, cha siew pau, loh mai kai*" – the lights would come on, one by one, on the tranquil street. Neighbours, clad in house coats, pyjamas and all sorts of nightwear, would come out of their houses to buy steaming-hot supper and catch up on gossip and chatter.

We were usually in bed by that time and our house would be all locked up and in darkness. Luckily, Grandma loved dim sum, especially *loh mai kai* – steamed glutinous rice wrapped in lotus leaf – and was often sorely tempted. She was usually the one to initiate the idea of a late night supper.

"Ah Soon is here. Anyone wants supper?"

"Yes! Yes!" we responded enthusiastically. The question was strictly rhetorical, of course.

Grandma would go to the window and call the Dim Sum man. Ah Soon would run over, take down her orders then run back to his cart to get the food. Excitedly, we watched Grandma, like Rapunzel letting down her long, long hair, toss her wicker basket tied to a rope out of the window down to the verandah below. Ah Soon would load the basket with the orders, give it a tug and Grandma would hoist up the basket with its precious goodies along with the bill inside, taking the utmost care while her grandchildren cheered excitedly behind her.

That night, someone must have pulled too hard. The basket swung crazily midway then got stuck.

"*Alamak, sangkut!*" muttered Grandma as she tugged at the rope.

We peered out of the window but couldn't see anything in the darkness. I ducked under Grandma's bed and pulled out her gigantic Ever-Ready torchlight. The basket had gotten entangled with the branches of the hibiscus plant in the huge terracotta pot in the driveway.

"Oi, Ah Soon, *tolong sikit! Dah sangkut lah,*" yelled Grandma.

"Help, it's stuck! Quick, quickly ah, we so hungry!" I willingly translated meticulously, though Ah Soon probably didn't understand a word of English.

Good-natured Ah Soon struggled to free the recalcitrant basket, watched by a small, growing crowd of onlookers. Eventually the basket sailed happily up to us, drooling like a pack of ravenous street urchins, to the cheers and claps of our bemused neighbours.

After the delicious supper, the excitement quietened down again and we went back to bed. I felt restless and unable to go to sleep. I had a strange, uneasy feeling, as if something was happening outside. Quietly I crawled to the peephole.

It was the strangest spectacle I'd ever come across in all of my ten years. I blinked, sat up, rubbed my eyes and knelt down to look again – I couldn't believe my eye. There was a gathering going on right there on the verandah – a gathering, of all the weirdest things, of cats. A cluster of around twenty or so of the most beautiful cats I'd ever seen. Usually when two cats got together at night, they were strays on heat, howling and caterwauling. These were definitely not tomcats on the prowl nor unwanted strays. Every one of them had lush, clean fur coats and looked very well fed.

They were seated quietly in a circle around the most magnificent cat, lying on top of our fraying coconut husk mat. They were of various types – I only knew how to recognise Prussian and Siamese cats – and in different colours of white, ginger, cream, black and tawny. The cat in the centre looked like the leader, a regal Siamese with creamy white fur, black paws and black nose. She was grooming herself gracefully, licking her paws and her body while the rest sat with feet tucked in or lay in peaceful repose. I couldn't hear any meowing nor purring from my height above. They were utterly silent and looked contented and thoroughly at ease, no spitting, hissing or catty histrionics at all.

There were only three cats in the neighbourhood – one-eyed, three-legged Ah Miau-Miau which belonged to the old albino lady renting a room at House Number 18, the mangy ginger tomcat at Number One forever trying to pick a fight with anyone and anything and Duchess, the friendly little kitten, treated like a queen and never allowed out of House Number 7. Our own pet cat Cocoa had died of old age last year. This was no ordinary phenomenon. I needed a witness. I stretched out my left leg and kicked my brother sleeping nearby. He was only six years old but he'd do, or else who would believe me, including myself!

"Hey, wake up, wake up! Shhhhh ... come and take a look."

"Owwww ... wha-aat?" he protested drowsily.

"Sshhhh ... don't make any noise, keep very quiet. Look."

He fumbled to the peephole and knelt to look. His body stiffened then arched in shock and surprise. He quickly withdrew and muttered,"Cats!?"

"Yeah cats! Ssshhh, my turn now." I nudged him aside.

We took turns to look in absolute fascination, when to our chagrin, the old clock on the bedroom wall started to chime the strokes of midnight. I gaped as I saw the "leader" get up and stretch gracefully. The others joined her, rising languidly and noiselessly to their feet. There were so many of them and yet not the slightest noise. It was bizarre. I wanted to call out to them, say "Meow" or something, but was totally transfixed in wonder. Then, just like that, they all got up and left, some jumping over the wall to the neighbour's and vanishing into the night. I couldn't see where they went given the limited range of the peephole.

My brother and I rushed to the windows – the street was clothed in darkness, the lamp post at the other end of the street revealed nothing, no cats strolling along, and not a bark nor a howl from the many dogs on the street. We went back to sleep, feeling as if we'd seen either a mystery or a miracle.

The next morning when I told my folks about the sighting, my mother scolded, "I told you not to eat three *cha siew paus* just before you go to sleep! Three huge buns, you glutton!"

"It wasn't just me! He saw it too. You can't have the same dream," I argued, pointing to my little brother, playing with his miniature plastic toy soldiers.

"Yes, I saw them too! And I didn't spit," he boasted, terribly proud of himself.

I was irate as everyone thought I was a drama queen with an overactive imagination and worse, getting my darling little brother to back me up. My mother, especially, was a voracious reader and knew everything, so I had expected a bit more intellectual interest on her part.

It was Grandma who pondered over my story a little longer. She pulled me aside. "There are many things in this world that can't be explained. Maybe they were spirits, *jinns*, maybe lost souls still traversing the earth, or ... maybe they were fairies, or even our ancestors, who knows?"

"Is that why you always tell us to *pai pai* ... to pray and say 'thank you' after we pee by a tree?" I asked curiously.

She smiled. "Well, yes, I suppose ... my parents taught me so I'm just passing that on.

"You can learn something from your experience with those cats. Respect all life forms, animals especially. You never know ... I don't have the answers. I'll only know after I'm dead and gone," she ended.

"Promise you'll tell me after you're dead and gone, okay?" I insisted, with no concept of the finality of death.

For years after that, I continued my dalliance with the peephole but never experienced an encounter like that night with the cats again.

Grandma died when I was twenty years old, reading law at the University of Malaya. I still lived at the old house with my family as the university was a mere forty minutes away by bus, and I far preferred the comfort of home to the university residential halls where I found the food unbearable.

I had a second supernatural experience in that same room with the peephole after Grandma's passing. Mother promoted me from my usual sleeping space to the spacious corner of the room where Grandma used to sleep.

"But ... but Mother," I argued, "this was Grandma's bed. She used to sleep here. What if ... er ... what if she still wants this space?"

"Don't be silly," Mother said, ever practical and realistic. "She's dead. The 49 days of mourning are over. We have prayed for her safe passing, she has accepted all the feasts in her honour. She is at peace, gone to a better place."

But evidently my mother wasn't so clever after all. For sure enough, on the seventh night, sleeping restlessly on Grandma's majestic Victorian brass bed with the hard plank base and squeaky springs, I woke up startled in the middle of the night. It was pitch dark but there, right next to me stood Grandma, a whitish ghostly figure without a defined shape, still in her usual garb: a little *baju pendek* top – a small blouse with two big pockets – and a sarong, all in a spooky white.

Her face was exactly the same, her hairdo too with her usual *sanggul* or bun at the back of her head, but the rest of her body sort of vanished into nothingness from the waist downwards. She was the same height and size and seemed to be floating suspended, right beside me. She stood there looking vexed and cross, as if trying to get into her bed but not knowing how. *And annoyed that someone was occupying it.*

I could hear her grumbling. "*Celakak! Gua mia tempat ni!*" (This is my space, damn it!)

"Ulp! Grandma! It's y ... y ... you! Err ... it's m ... me here!"

I was willing to vacate immediately but too petrified to move. Grandma hovered nearby, trying to figure out how to claim back her space. She didn't seem to recognise me but was concerned about why she couldn't get back into her bed and, I suppose, the world she had left.

"*Gua mia tempat ni*," she insisted.

I screamed, "Aarrrghh, go tell Mother that! She put me here!" and dived, terrified, under my blanket.

In the broad daylight now as I look out at my garden and reminisce, I still have pictures of Grandma in my head: stepping out of the bathroom *berkemban*-style in an old sarong tied around her chest, ambling to the second hall, pulling out a sarong from the cupboard and getting dressed there. Combing her long hair into a bun, she'd wear a lovely starched Pekalongan sarong under the casual one, securing it with a silver belt. Then she'd don a chemise and a matching kebaya. Making sure the kebaya was perfectly symmetrical, she'd fasten an *intan kerosang* to hold the kebaya in place. With one tug, the old sarong was removed. She'd then slip on earrings, her favourite *kasut manek* or beaded slippers, toss a handkerchief over her shoulder and amble out to the neighbours' on the next street to play *cherki*. I couldn't help thinking what a cushy life she led even though she didn't have a chance to actualise her secret ambitions.

Some encounters come only once in a lifetime. On that dark night, when she was atypically dressed all in white, I forgot to ask her about those beautiful cats, the memory of that childhood promise I'd made with her completely slipped my mind. Did she come back to keep that promise to me? What were those lovely feline creatures? I forgot to ask her.

I forgot to tell her I missed those wonderful late night suppers, her gentle ways, her lively banter and our conversations together. Forgot to tell her I had broken the glass ceiling on her behalf: She couldn't go beyond Standard Four, while I was the first in the clan to go to university and was on my way to becoming a lawyer.

Like the encounter with the cats, an encounter with Grandma has yet to return.

The Peephole is still there.

The House on Jonker Street

It was cold in the art gallery. The air conditioning was too strong. Nona decided it was time to go, she had spent far too much time here. The paintings exhibited in the Singapore National Art Gallery were a mix of brilliant pieces and a few uninspiring ones, nothing had really caught her interest. There was just one more room to go.

She stepped into the last room. It was long and corridor-like, painted an antique red, similar to the old Dutch buildings in Malacca. A single spotlight shone on a painting at the far end of the room. There was just that solitary painting in the whole room. Nona gave it a cursory glance as she walked hurriedly towards the exit. Suddenly, she stopped and froze for a few seconds.

She turned around in disbelief and looked at the painting again. Slowly, haltingly, she walked down the tunnel-like room towards that brightly-lit picture, an unseen force drawing her. She could make out the picture clearly now. She pressed her right hand against her chest, trying to calm her erratically beating heart. A gasp of recognition escaped her lips. It was a painting of an old house in Malacca. Her childhood home.

The painting was hauntingly beautiful, evocative of

another era when life moved at an idyllic pace. Of a Malacca that was no more. Painted in soft watercolours of browns, rustic orange and faded greens, it was a picture of an old Straits Chinese house, located along Jonker Street in the Old Quarter. Her home – her real home – was confined to a cramped little room upstairs at the back of the house, above the kitchen. The painting brought back a rush of memories, bitter-sweet memories locked away in a corner of her heart, never, she had thought, to revisit again.

She found herself lingering. The painting had a power over her...it stirred up images of her childhood days, unleashed forgotten smells and sounds. The aroma of thick black coffee, the crusty smell of bread being toasted on the charcoal grill, the rich redolent scent of custardy *kaya*, piquant sour-spicy *assam* curries, the *clack-clack* of mahjong tiles. She could hear chants and long-ago melodies – the knocking of chopsticks by the Fishball Soup man, the *tok-tok* sounds of the *Mee Sua* man, the clang of two metal rods by the Sticky Candy man, the calls of itinerant hawkers plying their wares along the street where she used to live.

Then, a painful wave of dark memories took over. Memories of hunger – raw and cutting, gnawing at her insides. The rumbling of her stomach, embarrassingly loud, triggered sniggers from her cousins. Meals were never enough. A cup of cold watery coffee and a slice of bread for breakfast, while her cousins had toast laden with strawberry jam, marmalade and butter, or thick satiny *kaya*. Lunch was non-existent – she had no money for meals at school, sometimes, a friend would share a sandwich or some biscuits. Dinner was a meal of scrappy leftovers, only after Aunty Cheng and her family had dined.

Every morning, the smell of toast would waft from the kitchen to Nona's room, tempting her with its delicate burnt smell. But she was never allowed to have any. It gave her Aunty Cheng pleasure to see the longing in the little girl's eyes, to enjoy the sense of power she held over her destitute relatives. It was the very first scent that assailed Nona's senses in the morning. The warm delicious smell drove her crazy.

What was it like? she wondered. How is it that cold sterile bread can smell like slices of heaven? How do those inviting pieces flecked with brown spots taste?

"Shoo! Don't touch it!" screamed her aunt when Nona once tried to furtively steal a slice from the grill. Her cousins smirked and grinned.

One day, Nona decided to beg for a taste of it.

"Please Aunty Cheng, please can I have a slice of toast bread?"

"What! How dare you!" her aunt responded scornfully. "Just be thankful you have a roof over your head. Nothing but a bloody blinking nuisance, you and your mother. Your father comes from a filthy rich family, so does your mother, and yet look where you are now! Of all people, I end up stuck with you two. I have to take care of you two parasites. What kind of *soey* luck is this? Thank your lucky stars you've got something to eat. Toast, your head!"

Aunty Cheng started screaming for Nona's mother. She found her at the back of the house, squatting by the big dragon-embossed urn, beside a pile of unwashed clothes, and shrieked hysterically over the splashing noise of water gushing from the tap.

"Margaret! Your stupid idiot daughter is giving herself airs! *Amboi,* bread is not good enough, now she wants toast. Who does she think she is? Ask her if she can pay for the electricity or not? It costs money to toast the *roti*, you know!! Who's paying the bills here? Greedy, ungrateful, good-for-nothing relatives. Bah!"

Aunty Cheng spat contemptuously at Nona's mother, then returned and pinched Nona, making her cry out in pain.

Nona remembered her mother grimly drying her hands on her faded purplish *samfoo* top with the daisy patterns. She pulled Nona upstairs into the privacy of their dark dingy room. Nona saw her mother brush her tears away furtively before she slapped Nona hard on her right cheek.

"Just remember, Nona, never ever beg for anything again. Do you understand? Work hard, do well in your studies and make something of yourself. Don't ever ask your aunt or anyone else for anything. I may have lost everything but I have not lost my pride."

"I just want some toast! What's wrong with that? I have

to smell it every day. Why can't I have just one bite? What's wrong with you all?"

Nona was young then. She screamed at her mother, then threw herself on her bed and sobbed into her pillow. She wondered why her mother was crying when it was she, Nona, who was suffering, hallucinating about toast, the one who had been pinched and slapped.

Nona never knew what toast tasted like her entire childhood, only that tantalising aroma.

The memory of that incident came back to Nona as she stood alone in the icy cold gallery, the stinging sensation of that blow, the emotional pain it must have exacted from her mother.

Nona's mother, Margaret, was born into a wealthy Peranakan family in Malacca. Her father owned several businesses including sawmills, an ice factory, a large property in Klebang, tin mines in Perak and several rubber plantations in Malacca. Margaret was his only daughter after two sons. She was vivacious, impetuous, intelligent and her father's favourite. She was adored by everyone and grew up believing that everything was possible in this beautiful, idealistic world. Educated up to Form Three, she was pulled out of school as her parents were worried that too much education would result in an independent, brash young woman, and she would not become a good wife. She had inherited her father's strong stubborn streak and this would eventually lead to a terrible confrontation.

With her dancing, expressive eyes, jet-black hair, slim figure and butterscotch complexion, Margaret was a beauty. When she reached eighteen years of age, she fell in love with a gentleman from a rich Peranakan family, the son of one of her father's business associates. Innocent and very much in love, she was blind to the fact that he was a playboy who liked to gamble and visit the bars and clubs in town, squandering his family's vast fortune. Her father refused to let her marry him.

"Please, Papa," she begged her father, "I love him. Please don't ask me to give him up. I won't."

"He is a playboy! It is well known in Malacca. He has no job, unless you call spending his father's money an occupation. He has not worked a day in his life. He is spoilt, arrogant and conceited. I don't trust him one bit. He is not the man for you."

"But Papa, you don't know him. He's not like that at all. You are just repeating nasty rumours about him."

"Margaret, I want you to be happy above everything else, you must know that. This man has a terrible reputation. He changes his women like the way he changes his cars. He has gotten two women pregnant – servant girl, cabaret girl. Scandalous behaviour! I don't want you to see him again. You deserve someone far better."

The charlatan playboy wooed Margaret secretly, used to getting what he wanted. Margaret, on a wild, romantic impulse – after weeks of trying to persuade her parents and an angry confrontation with her father – eloped with her amorous suitor one afternoon. When her father found out, he was outraged.

He sobbed privately to his wife, "How could she do this to me? How can she defy me like this? My Margaret, my only daughter, my life, my joy. Do I mean so little to her? Do we stand for nothing after all the love we've given her?"

He called his wife, his sons and the entire household together that evening and declared bitterly, "I disown her. She is never to step foot in this house, do you hear me? Never ever mention her name in this household again. From now on, I have no daughter."

Within a year, Margaret's marriage fell apart. Her husband, after the promises he had made that he would mend his Casanova ways, soon reverted to his old self. He began visiting his old haunts and indulged in one affair after another with singers and cabaret girls at his favourite nightspots. Even more exciting was the thrill of gambling. He indulged in endless poker and mahjong sessions, neglecting his young bride to whom he had made all those passionate promises of fidelity and everlasting love. Besides, she had become pregnant very soon after they eloped, wasn't very attractive to look at, and to him, not much fun to romance anymore.

One night, he came home very late reeking of alcohol, cursing with rage from his gambling losses and took out his fury on his wife. He slapped and beat her, blaming her for his bad luck in everything. Nona was just one and a half years old when her mother, unable to bear the humiliation any longer, packed up her few belongings, scooped up her baby and left. She could have returned to her family home and begged her father to take her back into the family again, but she refused.

"I will never beg my father to take me back. He disowned me. He lost a daughter that day, and I, a father. I do not have a father nor a husband anymore. I have you, Nona, and that is all I care about," her mother had told Nona once.

Her mother's cousin, Cheng, took Margaret and her daughter into her household. Aunty Cheng and her family were well-to-do but miserly and calculating. They took in Margaret and her daughter on the pretext of being charitable but in reality, Margaret became the household maid, assigned a heavy load of domestic chores. As time went on, Cheng grew increasingly cruel towards Margaret and her daughter. Cheng, the same age as Margaret, had always been jealous of Margaret's beauty, her hordes of admirers, her privileged lifestyle, and now took pleasure in humiliating her, lording over Margaret and her child at every opportunity.

Like Pandora's box, the painting opened old wounds, deep scars which time still could not erase. Nona remembered all those times when her mother came home from work, exhausted, her hands rough and callused, her lovely features slowly worn out with bitterness and hardship. Margaret worked as a washerwoman in several homes to earn money to pay for her daughter's education. After working all day, she would come home to more housework at Cheng's house. Cheng and her family members often made condescending and cutting remarks which Margaret had to bear silently as she had nowhere else to go.

As Nona grew older and became more aware of things, she wanted to hit back at her relatives — to answer back or defend herself whenever they made nasty remarks. The verbal abuse was unbearable at times, but her mother warned her to keep silent.

"Be patient, Nona. All good things will come to those who are willing to wait. You'll see."

Her mother's love sustained her. Nona was outstanding academically and at seventeen years of age, was awarded a scholarship right through university. She got a job immediately upon graduation. She managed to rent a room after a few months' earnings and moved out immediately with her mother, packing their few scanty belongings as Aunty Cheng screamed insults at them for being ingrates. They never returned to the house on Jonker Street again.

Nona scrutinised the painting. Perhaps she was mistaken, perhaps it was someone else's home. But she was certain of it – it was her childhood home. The façade of the house with its ornate stone carvings of birds, deer and squirrels. The familiar louvred wooden windows which she had to clean every weekend, the heavy ebony door, those colourful tiles with lotus patterns on the front porch, and the lamp hanging in the verandah. The black signboard with the family name in gold hanging over the door confirmed it.

Nona stepped out of the art gallery. A sleek metallic silver Mercedes pulled up in front of her. The chauffeur in a smart grey uniform jumped out and opened the door for Nona. She stepped into the Mercedes, leaned against the plush leather seats, pulled out her mobile phone and called her secretary.

"There is a painting in the National Art Gallery that I want to acquire. It's numbered 388 and is called 'A House on Jonker Street'. I want you to call up the gallery and purchase it for me."

Nona reached the grand Shangri-La Hotel in the city centre at 7 p.m. She walked into the Orchid Ballroom for an International Wine and Food World Gourmet event. Fellow wine connoisseurs came up to say hello to her. The Head of the Chamber of Commerce greeted her warmly with a big hug, while the CEO of Global Business Inc. rushed up to her side and attended to her every whim, signalling to the busy waiters to bring her a glass of champagne. The Ambassador of Ireland and his wife extricated themselves from their group to chat with her. Two socialites tottered by, dressed in designer gear from head to toe, exchanged air kisses and some small talk, then whirled away.

A waiter approached Nona, bearing a silver tray of canapés beautifully decorated, almost too artistic to eat.

Just then, her secretary buzzed Nona on her mobile phone.

"I'm sorry. I don't mean to disturb you but it is urgent. The painting is very expensive – more than sixty thousand dollars. There is another buyer bidding for it. Do you still want to buy it?"

"The price doesn't matter. I want that painting. Make sure you get it."

"It must be really special."

"Let's just say, I don't need it but I want it." Nona hung up.

The waiter was waiting attentively for Nona to help herself from the tray. Pointing at the canapés, Nona asked, "Tell me, what is this?"

"It is *foie gras* on toast with black truffle shavings, madam."

"Ahhh yes, toast! How delightful," Nona smiled as she nibbled the dainty canapé and sipped the champagne.

"Do you like it?" asked the French winemaker, curious about her reaction to his fabulous vintage champagne.

"Yes, I do."

"Ooohh *tres bien*, Madame. I am soh 'appee you are 'appee," he pronounced in an exotic accent, beaming with pleasure.

"I love the toast," Nona said, a faraway expression in her eyes.

"Ahh, the toast. Err...the toast?" the winemaker looked puzzled. "*Pardon*, Madame?"

She wasn't paying attention to him, deep in her own thoughts. She helped herself to another canapé. He shrugged, waved his hands in the air, and moved on to the next cluster of guests.

Nona excused herself from the circle of acquaintances and walked away to a quiet corner of the room. She nibbled the toast slowly, languidly.

Mother was right – good things do come your way if you are willing to wait. And work hard for it.

She thought of the perfect place in her multi-milllion dollar deluxe penthouse where she would hang her painting. It would look absolutely splendid there.

She noticed a crumb on her shimmering turquoise silk *cheongsam*, just beneath the necklace of South Sea pearls, intertwined with exquisite diamonds. With one beautifully manicured finger, she flicked the crumb of toast away from her bosom.

A very rich nyonya who was unmarried passed away and bequeathed all her property and belongings to her nieces and nephews. After everything was distributed, her dear friend who was the executor of the will found still more belongings in an old cupboard which no one in the family wanted anymore. I was surprised and delighted when she handed a piece of mauve Swiss voile to me one day with a beautiful matching batik sarong. She said, "Here you are, you are one person I know who will appreciate these."

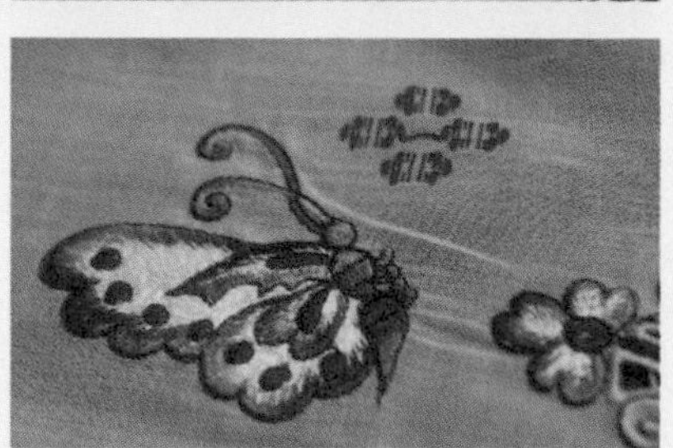

I gave the Swiss rubia to a famous kebaya maker in Penang, giving her free rein to design whatever she conceptualised. When it was ready, I was amazed at the craftwork. Aunty Kim, the kebaya maker, had created a wonderful luscious garden of blossoms, tiny flowers, buds, leaves and butterflies flitting about.

Dead Men Tell No Tales

"Never trust a man," said my mother, "not until he is dead."

I wondered why she said that considering her marriage was a fairly harmonious one. I was sixteen and not very experienced in the affairs of love. We lived at house No. 10 in a quiet street of old pre-war houses in a secluded part of town. There were just eighteen houses along that road, nine on each side. The occupants of the houses of Ceylon Lane formed a close community; everybody sort of knew everyone else living on that street.

Poh Lin Chee used to come over to our house occasionally to play mahjong or *chiki* with my mother. She was a loud, boastful woman and certainly not one of my favourite neighbours. Whenever my mother's friends made money at the mahjong table, they would leave a dollar note or a few coins on the table when they left, as a small tip for my sister and me. But Poh Lin Chee never bothered to leave any tips. We were kept busy the whole day long whenever my mother had her mahjong *kakis* over, serving tea, coffee, running out to the coffee shop nearby to buy snacks and just trying to be helpful, filial daughters. No wonder both my sister and I grew up loathing this game because it ruined our Sundays when Mother had her mahjong sessions. We hated the noise, the loud clackety-clack of the mahjong tiles as the mahjong players swirled and mixed them around, the staccato yells whenever someone pulled out a vital card, and the loud bantering and gossiping of the players stuck at the mahjong table for the whole day.

Poh Lin Chee was the bossiest of them all. She treated us like servants, totally at her beck and call, and conveniently forgot that we, too, were entitled to a life on Sundays.

"Ah Helen-*ah*," she would screech at me, "bring me some Chinese tea."

"And serve it in a proper Chinese tea cup-*ah*. Don't give me one of your mother's big fat mugs."

Or "Helen, Helen, come and scratch my back. *Aiyohh*, very itchy-*lah*. I am playing mahjong and you know-*lah*, I cannot stop the game and scratch otherwise everyone won't like it, so come Ah-Girl, scratch here...right side...just below my shoulder. Harder a little...a bit more...why so *boh lak* one? Ah Imm, you never feed your daughter-*ah*?"

"Ah Diana," she would command my sister, "go to my house and tell my daughter to take out the fish from the freezer. I want to cook *curry tumis* for dinner tonight."

I don't know how my mother and her mahjong friends could put up with Poh Lin because not only was she loud, she was unbearably boastful. Perhaps it was because for a really good game of mahjong, you needed four players and Poh Lin was the necessary fourth player.

Poh Lin was one of those who could not talk without boasting or namedropping. She boasted about her skills in running her household, her two brilliant children, her wonderful husband and her jewellery. That was all her life revolved around, but that gave her considerable ground to cover.

"My husband Ah-Simon is so good to me. You know what...you won't believe it! Last week he won a few thousand ringgit in the *empat nombor ekor* and he bought me a huge diamond ring. *Sui ga beh si,* so beautiful until can die one-oh...I wanted to wear it today, but then I am worried you all might scratch it."

She loved boasting about her husband's boundless generosity, how he was always showering her with jewellery and money, and how successful he was in his job.

"*Gua eh Ang,* he is so-ooo good, he always tells me to go and enjoy myself. Life is short, he tells me, and he gives me money to play mahjong all the time. He never controls my spending. I am so-oo lucky. I see you all always counting your pennies and cents. My Simon makes sure I don't have to worry about money. I don't even know how much he is earning. He is always getting promotion after promotion. I only know *chiak beh liau* in my lifetime."

What irritated me most was how she would go on about Simon's absolute devotion to her.

"My Simon, ever since he first laid eyes on me when I was an *anak dara...hee hee...*a lovely young maiden, he fell in love with me. He knew I was The One. Ever since then, he never looks at other women. Even now...*tee hee...*I am no more a spring chicken, but he is still crazy about me. In fact, he told me just the other day that I am even more better and more beautiful than ever."

Diana and I would sneak behind Poh Lin who was busy at the mahjong table, stare at the two prosperous layers of fat around her midriff, her double chin and roll our eyes in disbelief, while my mother, sitting opposite, would admonish us with a lot of eye twitching and eyebrow lifting to stop our antics.

My parents were happily married to each other. My father was a wonderful and devoted husband, but he never stopped looking at and admiring beautiful women. He was open and upfront about it, though, in front of Mother.

"Look at that beautiful girl passing by," he would whisper to Ma.

"Where? Oh, that one *boleh tahan-lah*, passable. She's too young for you, dear," she would tease him.

It was always done in jest but whether or not he lusted after other women, he never strayed. He was always faithful to my mother.

But still, Mother would tell me, "Helen, never trust a man. Never take him for granted."

"But Pa is so good to you, Ma. Why don't you trust men?"

"Hmmphh, that is because Pa's got no money. We are middle-class folks only and can get by. Now if he had tonnes of money, the women will flock to him, and then only will we know whether your Pa is good or not."

One day, I learnt what Mother meant. Poh Lin's husband suddenly died of a heart attack just after he had come back from an evening walk. Poh Lin was distraught with grief and wailed and mourned loudly throughout the two days of the wake.

On the third day, the cortege was about to leave the house for the cemetery. Relatives and friends had paid their last respects to the deceased, the hearse was parked up in the porch, the undertakers were getting ready to seal up the coffin when suddenly, a taxi came clattering around the corner and stopped in front of Poh Lin's house.

A young woman in dark sunglasses stepped out. She was short and voluptuous with a porcelain complexion. Dressed completely in black, she minced up the driveway in 4-inch stilettos. Her hair was bleached a coppery red, sprayed into a starchy bird's nest.

I was just a few inches away and noticed the thick foundation on her face. Her eyebrows had been trimmed to the point of giving her a perennial questioning expression. Her toe nails, painted a shocking pink, were incongruous with her mourning attire. A tinkling sound accompanied her every movement. It came from teeny bells dangling from a gold chain around one slim ankle. More gold glittered on her neck and fingers. I couldn't deny she was attractive but in a tarty sort of way which I suppose appealed to some men.

She walked in with an air of disdain, her strong perfume competing with the joss sticks and incense-filled air. The crowd of mourners made way for her, staring with mouths open as she sauntered into the hall in her high heels. She headed straight for Simon's coffin, snatched some joss sticks from the table, and looked around with a hint of a sneer at the simple funeral accoutrements. Devoid of any emotion, she began to light the joss sticks from the candles placed in front of a huge black and white portrait of Simon.

Poh Lin shouted at the woman, "Eh, who the hell are you? What are you doing here? Are you sure you got the right funeral-*ah*?"

The woman lowered her branded sunglasses very slowly. She looked up and down at plump, flabby Poh Lin in her cheap polyester *sam foo* and scoffed.

"Hah! So you are my poor Simon darling's wife. The poor fool. No wonder he was so fed up of you."

"What? What Simon darling? I am his wife. Who do you think you are?"

"I am his mistress," said the young woman.

"What?? Mistress! How? What! You bloody bitch. It's a lie!" screamed Poh Lin, blustering with shock.

"If you say so. He simply adored me, couldn't get enough of me. Poor Simon darling, he was just so sick of you."

Poh Lin screeched with anger and lunged at the young woman. The woman ducked, tottered on her high heels and fell onto an elderly man's lap. Embarrassed, the thin, balding old man smiled sheepishly and reluctantly tried to lift her off him.

"Oh sorry-*ah*, Ah Pek. I didn't mean to squash you," said the young woman, smiling sweetly at him. Placing two manicured fingers on his shoulder, she pushed herself up to her feet, her ample bosom heaving, her wiry coiffure completely intact.

Just then, another taxi pulled up outside. The clattering sound of the diesel engine grated irritatingly on everyone's nerves. The door of the taxi swung open. Everyone turned to look, and jaws dropped once again.

A shapely leg, clad in silky-black stockings and stilettos emerged from the taxi, a gold chain with little bells around yet another slim ankle.

PANTUN NYONYA JATI

Bungah telang warna biru
Tanda kueh apom bokkuah
Nyonya jati rajin poonsoo
Rumah tangga perintah semua.

Kain robia jait kebaya
Sarong batik pakaian Nyonya
Budaya Baba adat kaya
Ikut turut dewasa belia.

The butterfly pea flower is blue
Infuses the pancake through
The Nyonya diligent and skilful
Matriarch of the home she rules.

Robia voile sewn into kebaya
Batik sarong dons the Nyonya
The Baba culture rich & alive
Young and Old must let it thrive.

A *pantun* for *Kebaya Tales*
in honour of the nyonyas by
Baba Chan Eng Thai,
Peranakan Association, Singapore,
27 August 2010

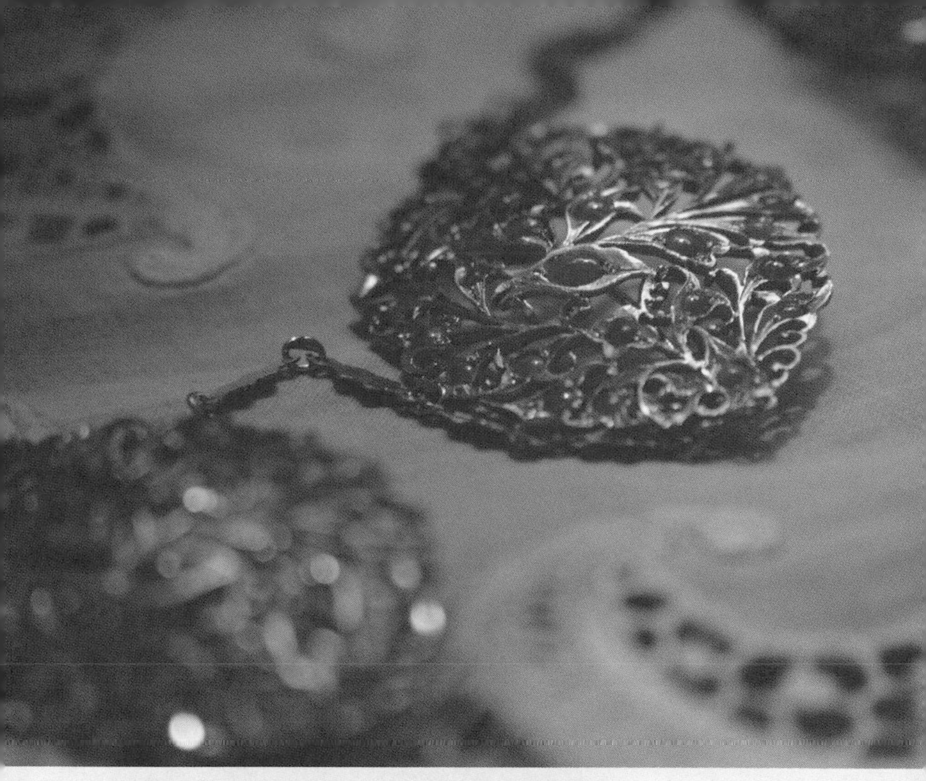

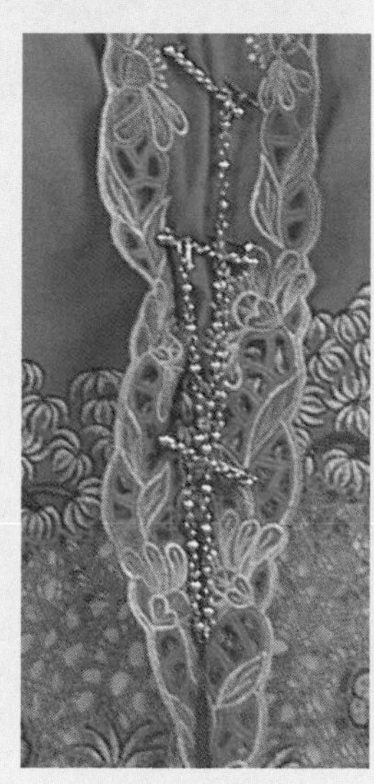

Kebayas are fastened together in place with the kerosang rantai, *three brooches connected to one another with a delicate decorative chain.*

The kerosang *was painstakingly handcrafted by Chinese craftsmen in the past. They were made of 22K gold and lavishly decorated with* intan *(diamond chips). Sometimes, diamonds or precious stones such as rubies, jade or pearls were used.*

Boxed-In Bibik

The Matriarch passed away at the age of eighty-nine. She was given a grand send-off in a lavish funeral, replete with banners, gongs, Buddhist monks reciting prayers for the safe passage of her soul, a five-night wake and a marching band.

"When they put me into the coffin, I want the band to play 'Taps'. My favourite tune. Don't you all dare forget," she had reminded her daughter-in-law, Janet.

"Such a sad sad tune...guaranteed to make everyone cry," she fixed a toothless grin at Janet and chuckled, looking quite pleased with herself.

"Remember, you lot. I want a nine-piece band, not a miserly three gig like what Si-Guat Neo had. I want a grand funeral. Don't stinge. There'll be plenty of money left from what your Pa left me," she nagged her children in her more lucid moments.

So the family had to look for a marching brass band. It was hard to find a nine-piece band – the local funeral parlour in Malacca had a four-man band comprising rickety, creaky octogenarians who looked as if one more puff on the trombone or trumpet would send them to meet their Maker. Finally, the manager of Kiew Kiew Blossom Nite Club & Cabaret at Jalan Bendera was persuaded to allow five members of his resident band to moonlight as funeral musicians.

The old lady had lived such a frugal lifestyle, it became extremely harrowing to certain family members that she got more and more extravagant the more ill and dying she became.

"I have already given instructions to Janet," she croaked to her family summoned to her bedside on yet another false alarm. "After I am dead, I want to be dressed in my most expensive kebaya – Janet knows which one – my best *kerosang*, and my diamond earrings. And my favourite slippers – the red beaded *kasut manik*. Don't anyone dare go against my wishes."

What?! Rosie, Daughter-in-law Number One, who had been doing a poor job of massaging the matriarch's bony shoulders, jerked upright, forgetting to maintain her staccato-like clumsy kneading for a full two minutes. She had hoped that Bibik's gorgeous *kerosang* – three delicate brooches of filigree gold metalwork studded with *intan* diamond flakes, linked by a dainty gold chain – would fall into her hands when the bossy old cow died. But now, the wrinkled vainpot wants to wear her three-carat diamond earrings as well! What next? Who the hell is going to look at her wherever the hell she's going? If the old loony went on like this, the entire family would go bankrupt. I didn't marry the eldest son of the family for nothing, fumed Rosie.

"And don't forget my gold anklets. I want to go out in style as they say...*heh heh*. And my silver belt – the one with the biggest buckle...make sure my sarong is fastened properly..., *nanti sarong jatuh*," croaked the old Bibik, enjoying her own bawdy humour, as she winked at Janet and glared at Rosie.

"If she lives another week, your crazy mother may decide to give everything to charity next. What are we to do, Boon Eng? You are the eldest son – do something!" Rosie complained bitterly to her husband that evening over dinner.

"What do you expect me to do? Can't you be patient for once? She won't be around much longer," he snapped back.

One Sunday morning, the family was summoned to Bibik's home again – the doctors warned that her time was nearly up. This time they were assured it wasn't a false alarm. They gathered around her bedside in the large dark room upstairs. It was gloomy and musty, smelling of clammy illness, alcohol swabs, antiseptic and Chinese medicated oil. But the beautiful stained glass windows, expensive art deco furniture and the many framed photos of the matriarch in happier times with her late husband dressed to the nines, including an autographed picture taken with a young Tunku in London, and another with a coterie of Sultans and British colonial big shots, whispered of happier and grander times in the distant past.

The old Bibik lay half-submerged in her king-sized bed, surrounded by pillows, blankets and hot water bottles.

She had tubes sticking in and coming out of her. Her colonoscopy bag – what she jokingly called her *jamban* bag – contained a few ugly streaks of greenish-yellow bile. She was still alert, her eyes darting about the room, her breath coming in loud noisy rasps. She kept pointing to something at the foot of her bed.

"I see two persons...there...in front of me. They are waiting. It is time to go," she mumbled, her hands trembling, her bony fingers jabbing in the air. Her large family of two daughters, two sons, in-laws, grandchildren and great-grandchild gathered around her, the womenfolk weeping and sobbing, the little ones puzzled, unsure, inexperienced with death's throes.

"My mother...she is waiting. Waiting for me, I can see her. Ma..."

Her relatives could see no-one but were edgy, frightened at the thought of an unseen presence.

Boon Eng, kneeling beside her bed, suddenly howled like a coyote in a cheap Western spaghetti movie. He grabbed her hand and plastered it against his cheek. The tragic expression on his face was limited to his twitching facial muscles, his eyes remained cold and unfeeling.

"Ma, Ma...don't go...*sob*...don't leave us. You are my... *sob*...everything," he sobbed.

His mother's piercing gaze would have frightened even Boon Eng himself had he looked up at her but he was bent over, shoulders heaving, trying to get his tear ducts to function.

"Ah my dear Boon Eng, always all talk but no action. *Tosa cakap lagi.* How much more do you want?"

She called for Janet, her favourite daughter-in-law.

"Janet! Janet, where are you? Bibik wants to say something to you," Rosie screeched jealously, flapping gratuitously around her mother-in-law. "Where's that sister-in-law of mine? You can never find her when you want her."

"I'm here," said Janet, standing quietly in the doorway. She squeezed her way through to the front.

"Ahh, Janet. Come here," the old Bibik smiled fondly at her daughter-in-law, and reached out weakly for her hand.

"Take good care of the house..." she instructed Janet. Then, her voice took on a strong urgent timbre. "You will clear up my room when I am gone, Janet? *Kam sia lu,* Janet."

"Yes, Bibik. Please don't worry about such things now," comforted Janet.

Rosie, leaning over to eavesdrop, smirked when she heard what Bibik was asking Janet to do. Ahh, poor Janet, ever the doormat.

Janet was married to Bibik's second son, Boon Guan. They both lived in the family home with Bibik. When Bibik became very ill, it was Janet who gave up her teaching job to take care of the old lady. Although Bibik had two daughters, they were not too keen to become caregivers, preferring to leave it all to Janet, their devoted sister-in-law. They made a big show of fussing over their mother when they dropped by to visit, but never went beyond shouting commands at the servants and giving instructions to Janet. Rosie would visit briefly, dropping in erratically to check if anyone was plotting to influence the old woman to change her will. The old cow had millions stashed away so you could never tell, just in case.

But Janet was safe, Rosie was sure of it. The guileless insipid thing. Not a scheming nerve in her brain or body. The unpaid Florence Nightingale. It was Janet who emptied the contents of the night chamber pot, fed and massaged the old woman, emptied her colonoscopy bag, administered the painkillers, tended to the bedsores. Yes, you can always depend on Janet, the woman with the eternal scent of Dettol.

Janet's cheeks were wet with tears as she reached out to hug the old lady and whispered, "Goodbye, Bibik. Thank you for all your kindness to me."

How strange, Janet thought, did the old lady just wink at her or was she grimacing from the pain afflicting her?

The matriarch looked at everyone in the room, her gaze resting a little while longer on her only great-grandchild. Her breathing became more intense and laboured. She sighed and closed her eyes. The matriarch went to sleep and never woke up again.

Hardly a fortnight had passed when Boon Eng's car came squealing up the driveway of the family home, and Boon Eng and Rosie emerged, slamming the car doors.

"Open up, open up, Janet," screeched Rosie as her husband banged on the wooden slats of the huge door with his car keys impatiently.

Janet dashed hurriedly out of the kitchen to open the door. Boon Eng and Rosie stormed into the hall.

"I want to know where my mother's nyonyaware collection is! I'm the eldest son. It belongs to me and Rosie now," Boon Eng demanded.

"Yah, where's all the crockery gone? Wah, don't simply quietly *sapu* everything hah! And where is the blue and white English tea set? The one with the Queen Elizabeth's head?" demanded Rosie. "Bibik said it's mine."

"Where's Boon Guan? Call your husband here, Janet, and let's get this settled. How dare you take my mother's things without asking me?" Boon Eng commanded Janet.

Janet was sickened by the wild accusations.

"What are you talking about? I have lived here ever since I got married. I have been using the same plates and cups and spoons for the past fifteen years. I haven't taken anything. You can take whatever you want. Just stop this nonsense," she protested.

Just then, Boon Guan stepped into the hall on hearing the commotion. "Big Brother, everything has been divided fairly and equally. What are you squabbling about? Mother is turning in her grave at your behaviour," said Boon Guan.

"Our mother's nyonyaware collection. Where is it? You think I don't know it's worth thousands of dollars?" Boon Eng snarled.

"The porcelain set is now with Eldest Sister. She took it. The English tea set belongs to this home. Janet has been using it all these years. What are we going to use if you take it away? Why are you behaving this way? Disgraceful," retorted Boon Guan.

Janet walked away, refusing to interfere any further. She could hear the two brothers yelling at each other and Rosie goading her husband. Just as Bibik had feared, greed was tearing the family apart.

Three nights ago, Bibik's two daughters had made a beeline for the huge mahogany cupboard where Bibik kept the paraphernalia for prayer rituals to her ancestors. The two daughters seized the two fabulous green and pink porcelain *kum chengs*, the embroidery pieces, the heavy brass candelabra and a huge yellow porcelain joss stick holder. They carted them to the boots of their cars and drove away speedily, terrified that Boon Eng and Rosie might drop in unexpectedly.

"Better take this home with me before that greedy busybody Rosie starts thinking it should all go to her!" said First Daughter.

"*Amboi*, the way she behaves, giving herself all kinds of airs. You'd think her grandfather owns the whole of Malacca. But no matter how hard she tries, she's just got no class! Did you know, Janet, her father is a hawker?

Fishmonger or pork seller or something like that!" Second Daughter dived in.

"Yeah she's so *kasar*...coarser than a butcher's wife."

"She's Cantonese, so she thinks her husband should get everything when Mother dies. Fat hopes she's got!"

"Too bad-*lah* for her, we daughters are equally important. But better hide all these first, just in case she grabs them."

One day, after another terrible row the night before between the siblings over Bibik's will, Janet decided to springclean the house. She remembered what the old lady had told her, almost her last words — to take good care of the house.

Donning an apron and armed with a bucket, a mop and a broom, she began a thorough clean-up of the family home. She started with her mother-in-law's bedroom. When she began clearing Bibik's cupboard, she was shocked to find that the old lady had hidden away stacks of money amongst her clothes. Janet found on the uppermost shelf two piles of stiffly starched Indonesian Pekalongan sarongs which Bibik hardly wore — exquisitely patterned, in vibrant colours of peach, sea-blue, mauve, green and reddish-brown. Slipped into the folds of each sarong, nestled between motifs of humming birds, phoenixes, swans, butterflies and irises were dollar notes in huge denominations.

There was more. Under the paper lining of each shelf, there were bills, dried jasmine flowers, receipts from goldsmith shops, and more dollar notes. Janet found more money – tucked away in envelopes in the chest of drawers, and bundles of notes tied up with rubber bands hidden in old shoeboxes under the bed.

Bibik's jewellery collection which she kept in a musical box on the dressing table had long been whisked away by her daughters but Janet found jewellery items bound in dainty lace handkerchiefs, stuffed in old brocade pouches under piles of junk.

Janet was stunned. Breathless, she sank onto the chair beside the bed, the chair which she had used when caring for her ailing mother-in-law.

She would have to inform Boon Guan and return all this cash and jewellery to the family. There was no way she could keep them. Brother-in-law Boon Eng would kill her if he knew.

Just then a little round box – one in which the old lady kept her potpourri, fell out of the cupboard. It rolled around in lazy, ever-smaller circles until finally, it ended right at Janet's feet. Janet opened the little box with trembling hands.

There were no dollar notes nor jewels inside. But there was a folded piece of paper. Janet rolled away the creases of the note. It was written in her mother-in-law's neat handwriting,

One last request.

Finders keepers, Janet.

Kebayas were worn with Pekalongan sarongs in vibrant hues. This green-turquoise sarong is filled with hand-drawn motifs of butterflies, birds, leaves and flowers.

Two vintage sarongs (previous page and this page) from my collection, both of which are more than eighty years old. This purple sarong belonged to my mother, and is typical of Pekalongan sarongs from Java which the nyonyas love.

The Bachelor from Balik Pulau

Lian was what they called an *anak dara tua*, an old maid. A confirmed spinster. She was plain and unattractive, with a morose and reticent personality. She spoke in a low timid voice, mainly in monosyllables. She spent her life entirely behind a pair of really thick glasses, so thick you could cut two table coasters out of one lens itself. Considering she hardly lifted a book to read, it was strange her glasses were so unwieldy and she, so myopic.

She was an orphan, adopted into a family who although was kind to her, treated her more like the maid than a daughter. But she could count her blessings, I suppose, for her adopted family took good care of her, though she never felt on equal terms with the rest of her sisters. She was educated up to Year Two of primary school then dropped out because of a lack of interest. She was always in the kitchen where she was most comfortable, peeling onions and garlic, grinding fresh chilli on the stone mortar, boiling medicinal soups, doing the laundry. Every afternoon, the neighbours could smell the overpowering aroma of *belachan* from Lian's kitchen, followed by the *tok-tok* rhythms of the *belachan* being pounded, for Lian's father loved to have *sambal belachan* with every meal.

Lian was in her early forties. All her siblings were married; she was the only one left staying with her father, a widower. Father was becoming quite feeble and frail, though he still liked to meet up with his old friends at the *kopitiam* somewhere in town. He would come back in the late afternoon and take a nap. Lian would cook the evening meal and wash up after dinner, then both would retire to their rooms. It was a comfortable arrangement, and no one would have thought it could get any better or worse. Until Ah Yang, the Second Sister, the meddlesome one in the family, decided to interfere with Lian's marital status, or rather, the lack of it.

One morning, Lian was in the backyard of the tiny terrace house, hanging up some sarongs to dry on the long bamboo poles when she heard Yang's Chrysler Avenger screeching to a halt outside and Yang flapping up the driveway, gasping excitedly.

"Lian! Lian! Where are you? Quick, quick. I have news for you."

Lian dropped the basket of clothes pegs and rushed out to the front hall, worried that something terrible had happened.

"What is it? Is everything okay?"

"A Man! A Man! I found a man for you," Yang blurted.

"A man? What are you talking about? I am not looking for any man," Lian replied, puzzled.

"A husband. I got you a husband," announced Yang dramatically, her double chin trembling with excitement.

Lian gaped at her highly excitable sister, a stir of irritation rising in her. Yang was always poking her nose into other people's affairs. Married to a rich, boring husband and childless, she lived in a big bungalow nearby. She had three servants, two Dobermans and plenty of time on her hands. Lian was annoyed that she of all people, was now the focus of her sister's interest.

"A husband, Lian. What more can you ask for?" Yang beamed, almost radiant with benevolence.

"What are you talking about? I never said I wanted to get married," Lian protested.

"My dear sister, this is a once-in-a-lifetime chance! Remember Soo Suan, our Klang cousin? Talk about fate. I bumped into her yesterday. She told me her uncle, a bachelor in his early fifties, is looking for a wife. Suddenly I thought of you-*lah*. Why not, eh? Surely you don't want to spend the rest of your life alone?"

Lian looked down at her hands. She was already quite alone and content with the way things were.

Yang added in a hushed, secretive tone, "Let's be honest. Father is in his seventies. He won't be around forever. When he is gone, you will be all alone. What is going to happen to you?"

Lian was not interested at first. She was indifferent to

men, love, passion and that sort of thing. She didn't even know what 'love' meant. In her entire life, no one had ever shown the slightest interest in her.

However, after weeks of persuasion and nagging by her sister, Lian finally gave in. She agreed to an arranged marriage on one condition – she wanted to know what her future husband looked like before she took the final step.

"No problem," said Yang, gleaming in triumph. "I will call Soo Suan to send us his photo."

"Photo? Hmmphh," grunted Father.

Father emerged from the tangle of newspapers he was reading and peered at Yang over his reading glasses, looking stern.

"Don't fall for that trick," Father cautioned. "My friend's nephew Teik Ho fell in love with a photo of a beautiful girl the matchmaker showed him. On the day of the wedding, he found out that his bride had a huge blue birthmark on the left side of her face."

"What happened?" Yang asked, shocked.

"What to do? Had to go on with the wedding-*lah*, or else lose face. Hundreds of guests already invited and everything paid for."

"Didn't the photo show?"

"No it didn't. The photo showed only the right side of her face. The beautiful part."

"Then how?"

"Everybody was furious at the matchmaker and the cheating family, while my poor red-faced nephew had to marry blue face!" Father chuckled.

Yang noticed the worried frown on her sister's face and immediately came up with another plan, determined to pursue her mission in life – matchmaking and spreading the joys of matrimony.

"*Eh eh*, I am much smarter. I won't fall for tricks like that, Pa. I will go with Soo Suan to visit this bachelor and check him out personally. No photo-photo business. See him in the flesh, *heh heh*, you know what I mean. Then I will come back and report to you all."

The next week, Yang called. It was all arranged. She and Soo Suan would travel up north to meet the potential bridegroom. The bachelor lived in Balik Pulau, Penang, and ran a little business selling cooking gas tanks. Balik Pulau was in a remote part of Penang back in the 1960s and getting there would require quite an arduous journey by train and by road into the interior heartland of Penang.

On the eve of her trip, Yang dropped by again at her father's home. Chin, the Eldest Sister, was also there to discuss Yang's trip to Balik Pulau and her matchmaking venture. Lian was busy preparing the evening meal, and didn't have much say in what the rest were planning for her future.

"I have to take the night train, second-class compartment, to Penang tomorrow. Inconvenient like anything," grumbled Yang. "I hate these second-class sleeping berths. These sick *hum-sup* lechers poke their hands though the curtains in the middle of the night and start groping around."

"Just poke their hands with something sharp. They're not interested in you, they're interested in your handbag. Now, Yang, coming back to this bachelor in Balik Pulau, I smell something very fishy. Why is he still not married?" queried Chin, the cautious and cynical one in the family. "Is there something wrong with him?"

"Oh, no. Soo Suan says he's a good man. Excellent husband material. Some more-*ah*, his business is doing very well. No regrets, she guaranteed me."

"Why can't he come down to Kuala Lumpur? Why do you have to go to Balik Pulau?" Chin frowned.

"He cannot get away from his business, Soo Suan told me. One-man show. Even for his wedding he can only take a few days off."

"Hmmm, I'm still suspicious. Check him out thoroughly. Make sure he isn't deaf and dumb, or missing some toes or fingers, or looking for a wife to cook and slave for him."

"Stop worrying. I will definitely make sure. This is Lian's only chance. Who wants her? She's getting old, not much to look at, her clock is ticking away. We are lucky someone wants to marry her."

Lian came into the dining room, carrying a tray full of wonderful sizzling hot dishes. Her hair was limp and oily after hours of slaving in the kitchen. Her simple cotton blouse had sweat stains from her armpits. She smelt of garlic, fish and prawns. Her face shining and dripping with sweat, she too wondered why anyone would want her at all.

Four months later, it was Lian's wedding day. She was dressed in a shiny white satin dress decorated with bows and frills on a long, flouncy skirt. It didn't really suit her but Yang comforted her that with a figure like hers, it was the best the bridal salon could do.

The make-up artist hired for the occasion was busy dabbing rouge on the bride's cheeks.

"Look up-*ah*, Aunty, while I putting on the mascalah," cooed the svelte make-up girl.

Lian had never used make-up before and felt uncomfortable. Besides, the comments by the so-called 'artist', young enough to be her daughter, were beginning to stress her.

"*Aiyah*, Aunty, why you no double eyelid-*wan ah*? Close your eyes while I drawing a line for you...*aiya*, donch blink so much, velly hard to draw-*lor*," the slip of a thing with the frizzy hairdo and tight jeans whined.

When her eye make-up was done, Lian fumbled for her glasses on the dressing table and put them on, to the dismay of the make-up girl.

Everything was ready. The house was all spruced up and spanking clean. A red wedding banner hung above the doorway, a long table was laden with delectable dishes, and all kinds of *kueh*, joss sticks and candles were lit at an altar to offer prayers for the couple's happiness. Relatives and friends poured in, filling up the tiny house, catching up and chatting away, waiting excitedly for the bridegroom to arrive.

Lian sat in her bedroom all dolled up, uneasy, her hands clammy with fear. Yang zipped busily about, gossiping with the guests, boasting of her success in marrying off her old maid sister. Eldest Sister Chin stayed with Lian, peering through the window every few minutes, watching out for the bridal convoy due to arrive at any moment all the way from Penang.

Children dashed in and out of the rooms, squealing with laughter. More guests arrived and wedding presents began piling up on the old *barlay*. The wedding *angpows* from the guests were stashed in a big plastic bag which Yang clutched tightly under her right arm. The house overflowed with guests and goodwill.

Yang noticed Lian growing more nervous and pale. The rouge on her cheeks stood out like two comical circles.

"Don't worry," she patted Lian's shoulder. "I told you I checked him out and he is fine. Not handsome-*lah*, but quite normal and a nice man. I didn't travel all the way to Balik Pulau for nothing!"

Suddenly, there was a loud hooting of car horns. Several cars pulled up outside the house. The first car in the convoy was decorated with strands of purple and pink ribbons and clumps of big silk flowers.

"Oh, he's here. *Lai leow, lai leow.* The bridegroom has arrived."

There was a flurry of excitement, a great hustle and bustle as everybody braced for the moment when the groom would step out of the car and come to claim his bride.

"Quick, quick! Where is little Boy-Boy? Get him to open the door of the bridegroom's car," screeched Yang.

"Boy-Boy, where are you? Come down at once from the rambutan tree!" yelled another frantic aunt.

The little boy was hauled ignominiously off the branches of the old rambutan tree at the back, propelled to the front of the house and coaxed to open the door of the bridal car. The groom waited patiently in the back seat, accompanied by his best man.

Annoyed at being unceremoniously yanked from his favourite pastime at his grandpa's house, the five-year-old stood beside the car for awhile, digging his nose. Then urged frantically by his mother, who dangled a rambutan at him, he finally pulled open the door of the big sedan, and stuck out his hand for an *angpow*.

Out stepped the bridegroom. He bent down low to get out of the car. He appeared to be quite big and tall as he had to stoop to get out of the car.

Everyone waited with bated breath, staring at this man who had come all the way to wed the *anak dara tua*.

Chin, watching from the window of Lian's room, pulled the curtains further apart, to get a better look at the bridegroom as he walked up towards the house, holding a bouquet of flowers.

Chin began to mutter, "Oh no, oh no...oo!"

Then a loud shriek.

"YANG!! Come here, you bloody fool! What have you done? Come here and take a look yourself!"

The bride was quite forgotten in the flurry of screeches and screams.

"What is it? What has happened? Let me have a look," Lian mumbled, turning even paler. She reached out for her glasses which the make-up girl had persuaded her to take off yet again.

Yang dashed into the room and headed for the window. Lian also tottered clumsily to the window in her cumbersome flouncy gown and high heels, and peered at the groom walking slowly up the driveway.

"*Alamak*! He is crooked!" gasped the bride.

"Oh God help me! He is bent over like a question mark!" croaked Yang.

Outside, everyone was stunned as the bachelor sidled up, grinning with joy that he had found a bride at last.

Father crashed into the room, yelling at Yang, explosive with anger.

"You got your sister a crooked husband! Didn't I tell you to check him out?!"

"I did, I did! I did everything, Pa. I talked to him, looked at his eyes, his ears, his feet. Even counted his fingers and toes. He was so well-mannered and such a gentleman."

She gulped for air.

"But...but..." it was Yang's turn to grow pale, "but now I remember, he never stood up. He just sat there all the time. His family members were running around, getting me drinks but...but he just sat there."

"Why didn't you ask him to stand up and walk

around, you idiot?" yelled Father.

"Yah, all of us are normal upright people and now look at you, *celakak*, you got some crooked type into our family. Told you how many times to check everything. Stupid!" Chin butted in, furious.

"How...how am I to know? He delivers gas tanks every day. I thought he was very tired," squeaked Yang, appalled at the humiliation she had brought upon her family.

With that, Yang fainted with a flabby, undignified 'plop' at Lian's feet.

Father looked at his daughter sympathetically, "Lian, you don't have to go through this if you don't want to."

Lian stepped over her sister's tubby body. She adjusted her glasses on her nose, pushed the veil away from her face. She looked at herself in the mirror. For the first time, she felt wanted – someone actually wanted to marry her. All her life, she had never stepped out of her cocoon. Here was a man, though slightly twisted, reaching out. That glimpse of him a few moments ago – that grin on his face – touched her heart.

"It's okay, Pa. Let's carry on," she said, "Let's proceed with the wedding."

And so the old maid married the bachelor from Balik Pulau. She really, really did.

Rumput pakis di tengah hutan
Bintang timur tergulong tergulong
Mintak jereki sebasar luatan
Mintak umor setinggi gunong

Ferns in the middle of the jungle
The Eastern Star flickers above
May your fortunes be as big as the sea
May your life as high as the mountain be

A baba *pantun* by Felix Chia, 1983.
"Ala Sayang!"
(Petaling Jaya: Eastern Universities Press)

This kebaya (above) belonged to my paternal grandmother, Ho Chuan Neo (left). Always impeccably dressed in baju pendek *(informal blouse worn by the nyonyas) or kebayas, she wore her hair tied in a* sanggul *(bun), never a strand out of place.*

Inside the innocuous-looking sanggul *lurked hairpins and an ear-digger, which she would occasionally pull out and poke the hand of whoever misbehaved, especially clumsy, bumbling nyonyas in the kitchen, whose preparation of food was not fine or* seronoh *enough.*

My paternal Grandma (left) and Grandpa, Lee Loon Chuan, with their two sons Koon Foong and Koon Liang (circa 1920s). My father is the younger boy.

My paternal grandparents outside our home in Sin Chew Kee Street, off Galloway Road, Kuala Lumpur.

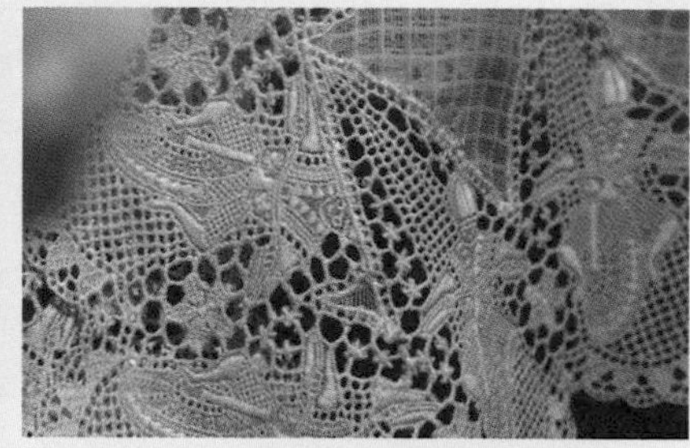

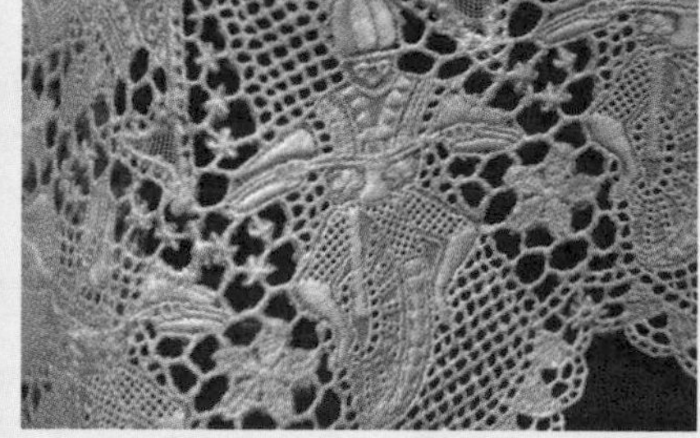

Me in my Grandma's white kebaya. This is the most cherished kebaya in my collection. I love it because it is dreamily romantic in classic white with exquisite lacework and an unusual embroidery motif – motorcyclists with crash helmets instead of flowers or birds.

The Breadman's Bicycle

She sat up abruptly and fumbled around with the bedsheet. She grabbed it in a bunch, turned it around and scrutinised it.

"What is it?" he asked, "Have you lost something?"

"Funny you should ask that," she said.

She had just lost her virginity but there were no signs of blood anywhere. She peered at the rest of the bedsheet...no stains, not even a spot of blood. Then it struck her – for some strange inane reason, Grandma floated into her mind.

Fiona started to giggle.

"Now what, my love? Are you all right? What is so funny? Or what, pray tell, was so funny?"

"No, no, it's not you. Nothing to do with you, *Sayang*... it's my Grandma."

"Grandma??" Russell looked really miffed.

"We have just made, I'd like to think, breathtakingly beautiful love and...and...you're thinking of your Grandma?" Russell questioned Fiona, his pride being delivered a terrible dent.

Fiona reached out and touched him comfortingly. "Now I know why she didn't approve of me and my bicycle...now I know why she always got so upset...she was afraid that I'd tear it..."

"Tear what? What on earth are you talking about?"

"And I think I did. Somewhere in between the cycling,

swimming, netball, tree climbing, all those sports, I think I did."

"I love you like crazy, but sometimes I really don't know what you are going on about."

When Fiona was twelve, her father bought her a bicycle. All he could afford was a secondhand bicycle which he bought off the local 'breadman'. In those days, bread was sold not from a bakery but from the bread vendor who cycled around town with all sorts of buns and loaves of bread strapped to a huge square bin tied to his bicycle. Fiona's bike was a man's bike, rather too big for her and when Fiona got on the bike, her feet could not touch the ground. It had a bar in the centre which meant that whenever Fiona wanted to get on the bike, she had to swing one leg high over the bar while the other gripped firmly onto the other pedal.

It wasn't the best looking of bicycles. It was old and rickety and the brakes weren't very effective. But Fiona loved it. It took a few days to learn how to cycle and quite a few cuts and bruises. But once she managed to balance herself on that huge oversized bike, she was overjoyed. She loved that wonderful feeling of tearing down the little hill near her home, the wind in her hair, the cool breeze brushing her face. Whenever she could find a clear stretch of road, she would race along it, revelling in that awesome adrenalin rush.

However, Fiona found it unnerving when every time, as she clambered onto her big breadman's bicycle, Grandma would stand at the verandah watching her and start muttering about how '*ta seronoh*' her granddaughter was. Grandma clearly did not approve.

"But Popo," Fiona teased her grandmother one day, "it is harmless. There isn't much traffic in our neighbourhood. It really is safe, Popo. Don't worry, I am not a danger to anyone."

"Ummph, *anak dara ta' seronoh,*" she would grumble. An unladylike young maiden was what Grandma called Fiona.

"What's *anak dara* got to do with it, Popo? I don't enjoy doing all the sissy stuff like sewing, crocheting and knitting which Sis likes. I love cycling, Popo, try to understand that. Why don't you like me getting on my bike?"

Grandma never gave her a straight answer. Fiona sensed that Grandma wanted to elaborate but seemed too embarrassed, or didn't quite know how to.

She would mutter, "I don't know why your father bought you this huge bike. And a man's bike too! It is so unladylike of you to *si kang kang* – open up your legs – all around the neighbourhood. So improper for a young lady!"

Before the bicycle, Fiona's favourite pastime was climbing trees. There was a big shady rambutan tree outside Fiona's home with sprawling branches just perfect for climbing. Fiona and her little brother would climb up the tree, perch on the branches and observe the activities in the neighborhood. Sometimes, they would imagine they were explorers sailing the high seas, looking for new lands to discover, or pirates scouring the oceans for prey to plunder.

Grandma's eyebrows would shoot up in dismay at the sight of her granddaughter swinging Tarzan-like from the branches, or clambering up and down like a monkey. But she did not want to interfere in her son's and daughter-in-law's upbringing of their highly-spirited daughter. All she did was to *tsk tsk* her disapproval.

It wasn't so much the cycling but the act of getting on the bike that seemed to alarm Grandma. Whenever Fiona pushed out her bicycle from the verandah, ringing the bell and beaming with anticipation, Grandma would watch her, her facial expression turning from concern to consternation. Fiona would position her bike steadily, place one foot on the left stirrup and ballerina-like, deftly swing her right leg over the bar. Then, hoisting herself on the saddle and wheeling off, she would wave happily at Grandma. "Bye, Popo. See you later, Alligator," and squealing with laughter, she would cycle away, a broad grin lighting up her face.

Grandma would grumble gently under her breath, "*ta seronoh budak ni*," as she ambled into the cool interior of her home, her beautiful brown Pekalongan sarong with the ornate red green and purple phoenixes and flowers rustling gently along with her.

Fiona remembered reading some time ago about traditional Peranakan weddings; grand, sumptuous twelve-day affairs where no expense was spared, they were laden with ornate rituals and ceremony. During Grandma's time, the marriages were mostly arranged marriages. Grandma herself never saw her bridegroom until her wedding day. She remembered reading about how, on the morning after the wedding night, the white gown that the bride wore had to be placed in a *bakul siah*, a lacquered nyonya basket lined with *bunga rampei* and fragrant flowers, and shown to the mother-in-law. If the bride emerged from her mother-in-law's house and sugar cane was tied to the car, it signalled that all was well and the bride's life would be sweet and harmonious in her new household. If not, the bride and her family would be disgraced.

Fiona sank back naked onto the pile of pillows on the bed. She looked out of the window and drank in the magnificent beauty of the view from the window. In the distance, the gleaming snow-topped mountains of the Alps lay before her. The sky was dazzling in its blueness, marked only by some white streaks of fraying clouds and a lone eagle soaring high above, riding the wind currents.

Unlike Grandma, she had married the man of her choice. Both she and Russell had been smitten with each other the moment they saw each other. He was English, and had come over to Kuala Lumpur to help his father run his vast tea plantation estates in Cameron Highlands. Fiona was a brilliant lawyer with a multinational corporation and was about to be sent to Hong Kong to head up the branch there when she met Russell at a party. A whirlwind courtship took place, followed by an elegant and simple wedding, and then off to the Austrian Tyrol for their honeymoon.

Now, all she could think of was her grandmother. The smile on Fiona's face turned into a wide grin, her eyes dancing with smothered laughter. Russell looked at her and thought he had never seen her looking so beautiful. Fiona tried to wipe her grin away but all she could do was burst into a spate of giggles.

Russell playfully whacked her with a pillow.

"What? What's so funny?" he asked, beginning to chuckle himself, so infectious was her laughter.

"Nothing, dearest. Don't worry, it doesn't concern you. It's something I have just resolved. With Grandma. She really cared for me, in her own way. And you know what?"

"What?" echoed Russell totally clueless by now.

"Thank God, your mum doesn't even care two hoots," Fiona smiled. "And look," she added, gazing at the soft cottony sheets.

"Er...at what?" asked Russell as his eyes tried to follow Fiona's.

"Look at the lovely whiteness of it."

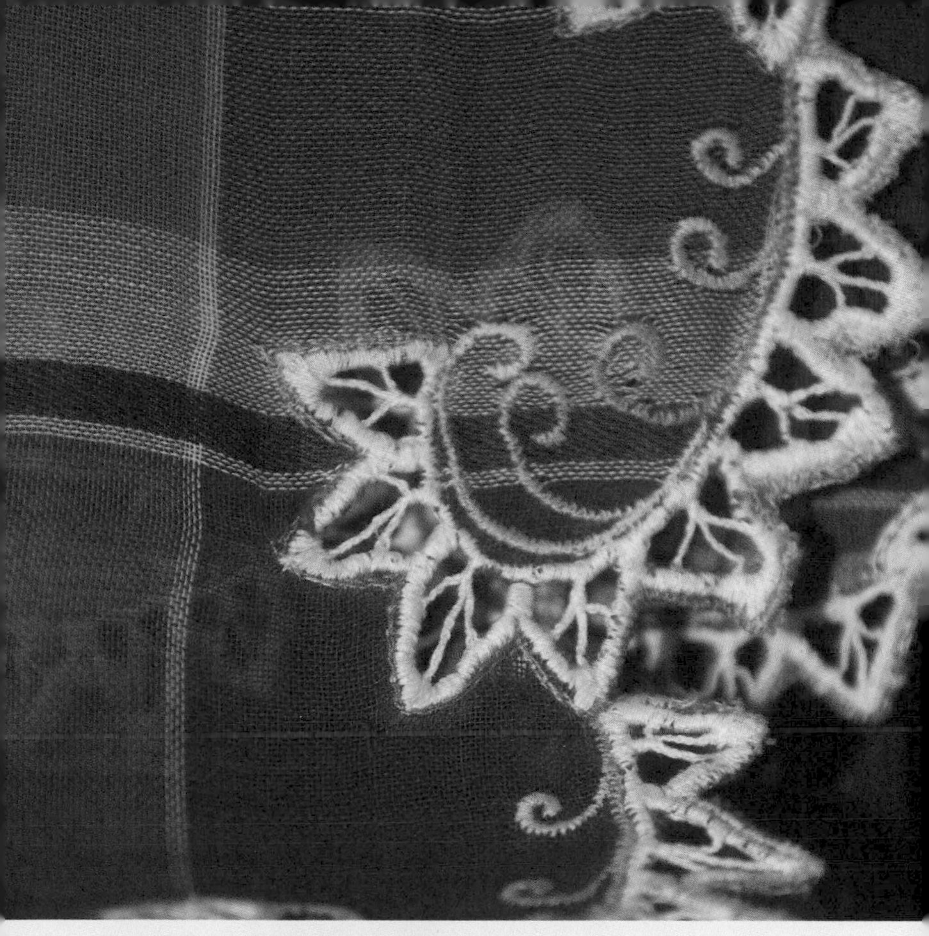

My mother, Kwee Hoon, loved the English language and literature and wanted to further her studies in Singapore. But the Japanese Occupation of Malaya in 1941 dashed all her hopes. For a long while after the war, she refused to buy anything Japanese until her last year at 66 years of age, she relented and bought a microwave oven made in Japan.

As kebayas were made of Swiss voile in the past, European influences gave a lovely touch. Apart from floral patterns, the voile sometimes came in checks. I inherited some kebayas from my mother who loved checks matched with simple scallop motifs.

Close-up of one of Mama's kebayas in white and red checks with centipede-legs motif.

The Goddess and the Japanese Officer

Scrrrr...unch...scrunch...SCRUN...CCHH.

Chua turned death-cold at the sound. Boots crunching heavily on gravel, voices jabbering in coarse guttural barks. He crept to the window in the front hall and peered out from behind the faded orange lace curtains. His worst fears were confirmed. He pulled back and crouched under the window, his stomach churning in terror. Marching up his driveway were three Japanese soldiers. Pointing excitedly at something at the front of his house, flushed and sweating under their caps with the handkerchief flaps, they were approaching fast, too fast for Chua to warn his family to run for their lives.

Had someone betrayed him? The radio was hidden away at the bottom of the rice bin in the store room. He had destroyed all the magazines and books, and burnt the photos of King George and the two English princesses. Why were they coming for him? When the Japanese invaded Malaya in 1941, Chua had hoped the horrific stories about the Japanese were untrue. Surely, for a people so clever as to outfox the British army, punch a gaping hole in the American armada at Pearl Harbour, such military brilliance could not come from a barbaric race. The atrocities committed in

Nanking and other parts of China must be just that – war propaganda.

Several months into the Japanese Occupation of Malaya, Chua found he was wrong, indeed, naively optimistic. The heads of entire families he knew, sat down to meals with, laughed and shared with, were now impaled on spikes in the *padang* of his old school, their eyeless cavities weeping trails of dried blood.

The crunching grew louder. The soldiers had reached the porch. They were just a few feet away. He could smell their dank body odour, hear their heavy panting. He braced himself for the inevitable pounding on the door, his teeth chattering in fear.

But the knock never came.

Puzzled, Chua gingerly lifted up the hem of the curtains to peep.

The three soldiers were praying to the Goddess of Mercy on an altar against the wall. Chua had installed her there when he moved into the house a long time ago. The serene, androgynous Goddess Kuan Yin, with her half-closed eyes, draped in light green robes, looked down benevolently at the Japanese soldiers with a hint of a smile. A lovely, beatific smile of happiness and compassion. Every evening, until a year ago, Chua would light a pair of joss sticks and pray to her for protection. How ironical that it was the Goddess herself who had drawn the hated Japanese to his home. The soldiers were silent in prayer, palms pressed together, eyes shut tight, bowing to her in deep reverence.

To Chua's dismay, they loitered around after that. One soldier pulled out a packet of cigarettes. The three soldiers smoked quietly, enjoying the peace of the spacious verandah with its blue-light orange Italian tiles and white balustrade overlooking the garden which was choking with weeds and wild creepers. One of the men was obviously the leader, from the way the other two bowed to him. Chua was so engrossed he did not realise the leader had seen him peeping at the window. He curled his finger at Chua, beckoning to him to come out.

This is it, Chua thought. This may be the end of the road for me. Maybe a slap or a few punches for spying on them or maybe a bullet through my head. Who knows? They had a record of being erratic and ruthlessly cruel in meting out punishment. Chua had no choice but to obey. Hesitantly, he stepped out, shivering in the humid tropical heat. Immediately, the other two soldiers sprang to their feet, hands reaching swiftly for their bayonets. Their leader barked an order and they withdrew, relaxing only slightly. The leader was tall, broad-shouldered and fair with a scholarly face. Chua thought he looked more like a genial professor than a military man in battle gear. His uniform indicated a very high-ranking officer. The other two were muscular and stocky, bristling with guns, swords and glittering bayonets. They continued to eye Chua warily.

The leader, pointing to the Goddess on the altar, asked Chua something in Japanese. Chua shook his head, uncomprehending.

The Officer struggled in broken English, "Pray, I wan pray."

"Pray? Er...what? Pray here?" Chua responded in confusion.

Do Japanese soldiers pray? Chua thought cynically. Pray for what? For forgiveness? Surely not even Her Holiness, the Goddess of Mercy would grant them that. The image of his sister, Bonnie, being dragged away by Japanese soldiers flashed into his mind. That ill-fated night a year ago. Dear, adorable Bonnie, always cheerful, too gentle to even step on an ant. Loved and pampered by all, the baby of the family, she didn't even know how to boil a pot of rice when she was taken away. Her terrified screams piercing the damp suffocating night, their coarse boorish laughter as they ripped at her clothes, the howls and frantic pleas of his parents as they begged for Bonnie's release – he could hear it all still.

He clenched his fists tightly. He had to focus on survival, he had a family to care for and he had to use all his wits to stay alive.

"*Hai, hai.* Pray here. This here," the tall officer pointed to Goddess Kwan Yin, "my God osoh."

The other two nodded. "*Hai, hai.*"

"I pray Bud...dha. Pray Buddha here. Good-*doh*. *Wakarimasta*?" the Officer continued.

Is he mocking me? thought Chua. Why ask for permission? Just seize the Goddess and take her home. Like Bonnie.

Chua struggled to stifle his anger and nodded. "Yes... er...I mean, *hai*."

The Officer smiled slightly and bowed curtly to him. The other two soldiers followed their leader and bowed to Chua.

What's this? Is this a trick? They are bowing to me. Usually it's us, the losers in this sickening war, who have to do all the bowing.

Just then, Chua's two sons, Ju Eng and Ju Kiat, three and five years old, burst out through the front door, bubbling with mischief. He could hear his wife's terrified screams from the depths of the house, ordering them to go back. It felt like a slow motion picture unfolding. Chua tried to grab his sons and push them back through the front door. They laughed and ran to hide behind the Japanese soldiers.

Their eyes widened when they saw the guns strapped around the soldiers' waists. Delighted at the prospect of new playmates, they pretended to shoot at the soldiers, cowboy-style.

"Bang!" squeaked chubby little Ju Eng, his fat thighs wobbling. "Die, *Jipoona kui*!" repeating one of the many Hokkien curses he had picked up from his mother.

"Boys, get inside the house NOW!" Chua tried to speak calmly, gritting his teeth.

Ju Kiat, the older boy, imitated what he had often seen the Japanese soldiers doing to their unfortunate victims. "*Bakelo!*" he yelled and kicked the shin of the tall officer.

Chua stood transfixed, his blood draining out of him.

The Japs would surely kill them all now.

He saw the Officer reach swiftly for his gun tucked in his belt. He pulled out the gun and pointed it at Ju Kiat, who reached up to his mid-thigh level. The gun was just three inches away from his son's head. Ju Kiat looked up and smiled innocently at the Officer. Chua was about to throw himself in front of his son when he heard the Officer say,

"Bunng!"

The boys squealed with laughter and shot back, "Bang! Bang!"

The Officer beamed happily, his eyes lighting up with childlike enjoyment. He looked at the two tiny boys running around and started laughing.

"Bang! Die, Die. You die!" yelled the boys.

"Bungg!" the Officer responded, "Ha ha ha, Bung, Bungg!"

Ju Eng collapsed on the floor with a dramatic *Arrrgghh*.

The Officer laughed till tears rolled down his cheeks, slapping his thighs and clutching his tummy in mirth. The other two soldiers laughed nervously, aping their leader. The Officer picked up Ju Eng and tossed him in the air as the little boy screamed excitedly.

Chua's wife rushed out and grabbed Ju Eng from him, snarling like a tigress. The Officer's eyebrows shot up in surprise at her unexpected appearance, at her almost unhinged expression, eyes flashing, hair flying behind her. Chua's heart stopped beating for a moment, gaping in dismay at her effrontery to the Japanese. The Officer's lips twitched a little — as if amused at her feisty behaviour.

"Give me back my son! Don't you dare touch my boys," she hissed.

Eyeing the Japanese soldiers defiantly, she shoved the boys into the house.

"Ju Eng, Ju Kiat, get inside! Now, this very minute!" she commanded.

The Officer bowed politely to Chua's wife, while she eyed him coldly, unable to hide her loathing and disgust. The two soldiers looked at their leader expectantly for instructions, their fingers clasping the hilts of their swords automatically. Chua, speechless with disbelief that he and his family were still alive, noticed a softness in the Officer's expression as he stared wistfully after the two boys.

The Officer pulled out something from his military jacket — a scroll with some Japanese words. His men plastered it on the front door. Bowing once more to the Goddess, the Officer and his men marched away down the driveway.

Chua peered at the scroll. The Japanese characters were emblazoned in black against a red background. He left it alone, rankled at its presence, but too afraid to remove it. It served a powerful function, Chua found out soon enough.

Chua's house was on the main road. A number of Japanese platoons marched by every day. Whenever Japanese soldiers saw the scroll, they would bow respectfully and walk away. No Japanese dared venture near nor harm Chua and his family.

One night, a troop of drunken Japanese soldiers stomped up the driveway searching for women, yelling "*ku nian, ku nian*",pounding on the door, shining their torches. When they saw the scroll, they skulked away.

Over the next two years, the Officer would drop by occasionally to worship the Goddess at Chua's place. Sometimes, he would disappear for months then suddenly turn up with a bag of rice. Chua was grateful as rice was a rare commodity during the Japanese Occupation. His family was sick of tapioca, the staple food but it was better than starvation. Chua sometimes invited the Officer into his home for a drink. There was something about the gentle-mannered Officer which Chua liked and trusted instinctively. A strange sort of friendship developed. The Officer enjoyed his visits, savouring the quiet solitude, sipping tea and making minimal conversation with Chua, using gestures and a sprinkling of Japanese and English. He liked to look at the books on Chua's bookshelf, running his fingers over the pages, unable to read the words in English but enjoying himself nevertheless.

The Officer adored Chua's two sons. They, in turn, enjoyed playing with him, clambering and tumbling about in physical play. Chua's wife was uncomfortable and nervous during his visits but kept her peace. The Officer would place his weapons on the table in the front hall, then go down on all fours and play with the boys. Once, Chua found them rolling on the floor in laughter near the table. Delicately, he picked up the Officer's heavy Samurai sword and put it away on the top shelf of the bookcase with a grimace, wondering how many heads it had sliced off.

One morning, after a long absence, the Officer appeared unaccompanied at Chua's porch, ashen-faced and dishevelled, his hair uncombed, his clothes crumpled. He had been walking for a long time, his shoes and his pants were covered in mud. He stood at the front door, looking dazed. Chua was puzzled, for the 'General', as Chua called him, was always composed and impeccably dressed.

He staggered in and slumped onto a chair.

"What is it, General? What has happened?"

The Officer did not respond, struggling to keep his face impassive. Then he broke down, burying his face in his hands in anguish. He wept as if his whole world had collapsed around him, a terrible sorrow wrenching him apart. His body racked with sobs which he tried hard to suppress. He rolled his head in his hands, moaning softly like a wounded animal.

Chua was stunned. Had the Allies won the war? Were the Japs finally relinquished?

"General, are you alright?"

"Chua-*san*," he mumbled, "My...my..."

He paused, unable to find the words. His eyes searched the room. He saw the portraits of Chua's parents on the wall. His shaking hands pointed at the sepia-tinged faces gazing solemnly down at them.

Chua's eyes followed the Officer's.

"Er...those are photos of my parents. My father and mother. They're both dead. Killed by the...er...I mean... killed in the war," Chua said.

"My Fah-duh Mah-duh osoh dead," the Officer intoned dully.

That makes it even, Chua thought, ashamed at his callowness. Although I'm sure your parents died peacefully, perhaps of old age or dementia. My mother died of a broken heart, crying out for Bonnie. My father never got over that. He was beheaded for spitting at a troop of Japanese soldiers when they ordered him to bow to the Nippon flag. His head was up for display at the school *padang* not too long ago.

The Officer continued, his voice quavering, "My w... wi...wife osoh dead."

He pulled out a photograph from his pocket and pointed at a Japanese woman and two little boys seated beside him in the photo.

He sobbed, "My wife Eriko dead. My...how you say... my love...my Eriko."

Chua gripped a chair for support. The Officer went on. "My two son...osoh dead."

Chua scrutinised the photo. The Officer's two sons looked just like his own boys – the same age and size, even similar crewcut hairstyles. They were dressed in white shirts and little bow ties, both grinning, eyes sparkling, staring cheekily at the camera. The woman in the photo was fair and delicate with high cheek bones and soft sad eyes, dressed in a beautiful kimono with storks and rainbow patterns.

The Officer croaked hoarsely, “My two boy, Koji and Tomi, dead. My...my two son.”

“Hiroshima dead. All, all dead,” he continued.

Chua shook his head in disbelief, unable to say anything to commiserate.

The Officer went on, mechanically,”Nagasaki osoh dead. Many, many die.”

“I die too. I die inside,” he finally ended his long litany. The Officer rocked back and forth, tears streaming down his face.

“General, I...I am so sorry. I don’t know what to say,” said Chua, horrified at the tragedy that had befallen his unlikely friend.

What did it all mean? Hiroshima? Nagasaki? Were they people, relatives of the Officer? Or were they places? They sounded like places to Chua. Was this the end of the war then? Or just another tragic turn? Chua found himself crying too. Crying for he knew not what...for himself, for the General, for the terrible cost of war. Images of his parents, his brilliant and affable Papa whom he adored, Ma with her charm and razor-sharp wit, his sister Bonnie, his friends and family members killed in the war, the Officer’s wife and two sons – their faces floating hauntingly in his head, disembodied, merging into each other, forming a knot of unbearable sorrow. The Officer and Chua sat there for a long time in silence. Finally, wiping away his tears and bracing his shoulders, the Officer got up to go. Before he stepped out of the house, he bowed deeply.

"Chua-*san*, I no come back. No more. *Sayonara.*"

"Goodbye, General. But when the war is over, who knows? Perhaps one day, we will meet again."

The Officer shook his head adamantly, "No. No more. I no more soon."

Chua didn't know what the officer meant.

At the porch, the Officer paused in front of the Goddess of Mercy. He bowed low then marched down the driveway for the last time, his right fist clutching his Samurai sword till his knuckles gleamed a pale white in the sunshine.

"Goodbye, General," whispered Chua. "I don't even know your name. We could have been good friends in happier circumstances."

Chua watched the Officer disappear slowly out of sight. The scorching sunlight was hurting his weary eyes. As he was about to retreat into the cool darkness of his house, he stopped, stunned by a revelation. He turned and stared at the Goddess sitting serenely on her perch.

She was still the same Goddess of Mercy figurine, tranquil as ever with the beautiful smile. Only, for the first time, it occurred to him that he had misinterpreted the expression on her face all along. It wasn't a smile of happiness after all, but a smile of sorrow. A grimace almost of infinitesimal sadness at this sordid, cruel world.

Kebayas come embroidered in three ways: kebaya biku *which are simple embroidery in the shape of scallops or* ombak *(waves),* sulam penuh *(full embroidery) and* sulam kerrawang *(cut-through embroidery).* Kebaya rendas *are trimmed with European lace, purchased from the door-to-door* 'kling tong' *man or haberdasher.*

The nyonyas love flower and aninal embroidery motifs and French or English lace to decorate the edges and hems of their kebayas.

My Old Baby

When Michael was born, I had this strange feeling it wasn't the first time he had come into this world. He didn't cry when he first appeared after twenty-two hours of labour. The doctor had to give him a whack on his bum which made him bawl a bit. The nurse hastily wiped the mucus and blood off him and gently laid him on my chest.

"It's 5.10 a.m. and you have a baby boy."

I looked in wonder at the tiny thing sitting cross-legged on my bosom, its head wobbling like an Indian classical dancer. It had been a harrowing battle bringing him into the world.

I whispered, "Hi Michael, it's me, your Mama."

At the sound of my voice, his unfocussed gaze drifted to me and he blinked several times. He tilted his head and stared. A tiny twitch of his lips as if in recognition, a yawn, and then, a strange grumpy expression of, "Oh well, here we go again."

I ran my finger over his forehead, his tiny nose and mouth. He looked weary and all crinkled up after his long struggle. His baldness except for a clump of fine, wavy hair on the top of his head made him look like a wrinkled old gnome. There was still some dried blood on his forehead. He wasn't the cute winsome baby I had expected but he was still my baby and I loved him dearly.

Apart from his usual needs, my newborn hardly gave any trouble. He was like a polite gentleman who didn't want to be a bother. Even when breastfeeding, I felt his discomfort that he was being an imposition on me.

I would coo, "C'mon, my little baby, drink your milk."

I would gently thrust an engorged nipple to his lips. Instead of sucking hungrily, he would look away, a little embarrassed. Finally, he would comply and suckle, but only for a while. This was always such a struggle I gave up after two months.

At the age of ten months, he suddenly got up and started walking. Speaking took a little longer. He didn't talk until he was two and a half years old which worried my husband and I considerably, but once he started, he spoke coherently, proper words and not baby language.

He was a child and yet, not really. At the playground, he refused to join his peers. He sat in his stroller looking thoroughly bored with the business of growing up. Occasionally, he would get up and walk around like a watchful headmaster, hands folded behind him, shoulders stooped, an eyebrow shooting up anxiously whenever he chanced upon a child playing too boisterously on the swings or the see-saw.

When I asked him why he didn't play with the children, his reply was, "Play? What for?"

One day, when he was four years old, I brought Michael along to visit an old school friend, Junie, who lived in a pre-war shophouse on Temple Road. Junie invited me upstairs to the family's living quarters for tea.

As we navigated the dark narrow staircase, Michael suddenly grabbed my skirt and clung to my legs, almost making me lose my balance.

"Michael! Please stop it. Walk properly."

"Mama, I don't want to go upstairs. Get away from me, you ugly thing."

"Who's ugly, Michael? Stop clinging to me. I can't walk."

"What's the matter, Michael? Come upstairs, don't be shy, Aunty has got lots of cakes and sweets for you," Junie tried to soothe Michael.

"I don't want any. I want to get out of here!" he yelled.

Later, when driving home, I asked him to explain his rude behaviour.

With a shudder, Michael said matter-of-factly, "A dwarf, Mama. An ugly dwarf at the bottom of the staircase. He didn't like me. He was very angry."

"A what? A dwarf? You mean dwarf as in *Snow White and the Seven Dwarfs*!?

"That's the fairytale. This dwarf was sitting right there. He's nasty."

I stared, perplexed, at my child. Had he been watching too much TV? Or worse, was he one of those who could see the spirit world? I had heard of such people before – clairvoyants, mediums, people who saw ghosts, demons, *toyols* or little dwarf spirits. Was this a blessing or a curse? Of all people, for God's sake, why my son?

Another time, on a trip to the East Coast of peninsular Malaysia, we stopped at a rest house in Kerteh in Terengganu. Michael sensed an unseen presence the moment we entered the main hall. He refused to go any further. His father thought Michael was throwing a tantrum and scolded him. Not wanting to displease his father, Michael finally walked in hesitantly.

A cold shiver tingled through me when I heard my son speaking to no one in particular.

"We come in peace, we are here for just a while. Don't harm my mama and papa. We will leave soon."

His head was lifted up high as he was speaking. Whoever it was, I thought, he must be really huge, at least six feet tall. Michael refused to stay the night there and insisted we leave immediately. Later that night, Michael climbed into bed with us, refusing to sleep alone.

"What did you see in the rest house today, Michael?" I asked him.

"He's huge, Mama. And evil and dark."

"Who, Michael?" I asked, my stomach contracting in fear.

"The man living there. He was murdered. He wanted to harm us."

Michael started to cry softly until he went to sleep.

I discussed Michael's odd behaviour with my husband, Khon Beng, one evening.

"He's not quite normal. I'm worried. He doesn't play with other children. He is always a loner in school. He sees and hears things that we can't. He is like an old person inside a young boy's body."

"Must be from your side of the family," my annoying hubby teased me. "I always thought your Aunty Pek Nya was weird, especially on full moon nights. Any lunacy in your family?"

"Stop kidding. What are we going to do?"

"Just treat him like a normal person. Just our bad luck. If only Michael can predict *empat nombor ekor* or the winning lottery ticket, that's so much better than seeing ghosts and the devil," my perennial joker of a husband said.

I glared at my husband in exasperation. And continued brooding about Michael.

It was on a trip to Port Dickson that my suspicions about my son were more or less confirmed. We had spent a restful break at a chalet at 5th Mile, and were homeward bound on the old Port Dickson road to Malacca. Passing by endless rows of rubber trees, I saw an unfamiliar flash of blue. The sunshine glinted through a break in the hypnotic parade of trees. I braked my car gently – we saw a path in the dark brooding rubber estate leading towards that enticing blueness.

I had never seen the path before, although I had driven along the coastal road countless times.

"Shall we explore?" I asked the rest. "I think I caught a glimpse of the Straits of Malacca from here."

There were five of us in the car – my best pal, Geraldine, her two teenage girls, Michael and I. The path wound through the gloomy estate and ended in a clearing. There, right in front of us was a beautiful secluded beach, hemmed in by promontories covered in forest and shrubs. The turquoise-green sea was deadpan calm, its waves breaking in noiseless crinkles.

"This is a charming place. Let's picnic here," Geraldine suggested.

We tumbled out of the car and strolled to the beach. I pulled out my camera and started taking photos. The two girls dashed into the sea and splashed around in the water. Geraldine had brought along a Thermos flask of coffee and some sandwiches. We sat on the fine white sand and relaxed, enjoying the piping hot coffee.

As Geraldine chatted away, I became aware of a stifling oppression in the air. It must be the humidity of the morning, but it intensified with every minute.

"Shhhhhh! Hush," I cut Geraldine off.

"Whatsamatter?"

"Listen, Geraldine. There's something weird going on here. This place is absolutely quiet. I don't hear any birds, no cicadas, no chirping, no sound at all."

"Why? Should there be noise?"

"It is as quiet as death."

"Yeah, come to think of it, the only noise is us. It's bizarre."

"It feels creepy here. Let's finish our coffee and get out of here. Where's Michael?"

I spotted him near the car, squatting on the sand.

"Hey girls, get out of the water. We are moving on," yelled Geraldine to her daughters.

The girls waded out of the sea, their T-shirts all wet and clingy, laughing happily. I stole a glance at Michael as we got into the car — his face was pasty-white and he was trembling with an inexplicable horror at something. I had no desire to ask him what he saw this time.

I sent the film for processing soon after the trip. I forgot all about the eerie place until I saw the photos. I was shocked at what I saw.

There were slit-shaped pairs of eyes in every photograph taken at that beach where we had picnicked. Malevolent, glinting with hatred and vengeance, the eyes looked evil. A cluster of them hovered near the two teenage girls, some almost touching them, leering at the girls' firm young bodies. One pair was plastered in gleeful delight at the elder teenager's right breast. Behind them were more eyes gathered in a semicircle. A few thronged around Michael, filled with intense wrath. They were all over the beach in every photo, a small army of disembodied eyes, gleaming with a frightening brightness, awakened from a long lull.

The other photos from the same roll of film were fine, only those taken at that beach had these intensely evil eyes dancing all over them. I called Geraldine to come over immediately.

Geraldine was scared. I told her I didn't think it had anything to do with the quality of the film.

"Those eyes," she shuddered, "they look vile."

"I think we stumbled onto a really bad place. Those eyes are human eyes, I'm sure of it. I think they belong to spirits, dead beings roaming on that beach that morning, Geraldine," I said.

"What on earth are you talking about?"

I told Geraldine about Michael's strange ability to see spirits and how he looked terrified out of his wits that morning.

"Well, did you ask him what he saw? Maybe he can tell us what these strange things belong to!"

"I was too afraid to ask. I just didn't want to know," I said.

"What shall we do with the photos?" asked Geradine, looking really worried.

"We've got to destroy them. Somehow the film has captured the images of these spirits. We've got to release them."

Geraldine agreed. We made a bonfire in the backyard and threw in the photos. We watched the photos curl up in the flames, reduced to a pile of black ashes.

Just then, Michael appeared.

I told him sharply, "Go away, Michael. Mama and Aunty Geraldine are busy here. Please go back into the house."

"Mama, you have forgotten something," Michael said.

"What, Michael?" I asked, feeling irritated, edgy, haunted by those vindictive eyes.

"The negatives, Mama. Destroy the negatives."

"What? Oh yes, the negatives!"

"Quick! Get rid of them!" urged Geraldine.

I ran into the house and pulled out the envelope containing the negatives. I dashed out into the backyard and tossed them into the fire. As the negatives burned, angry hisses emanated from the fire.

Was I imagining or did I actually see narrow slit-like shapes darting up from the fire? They hovered above the crackling flames for a few seconds, looking angrily in all directions, the slits narrowing even more till they became thin lines of pure evil, then with angry crackles, they disappeared into the air in hissing snarls as the ashes curled upwards in the breeze.

Michael came up to me and put his little hand in mine.

"They're gone, Mama," he said.

As we walked towards the house, I asked Michael hesitantly, cringing with dread.

"Michael, what...what exactly did you see that morning at the beach in Port Dickson?"

"There were many spirits there. They were soldiers. Speaking a strange language. They committed suicide there. They are restless and unhappy, they can't go home. They have not found peace, Mama."

I grasped my little boy by his frail wraithlike shoulders and looked deep into his eyes, those limpid light brown eyes of an old, old soul.

I asked him gently, "Who are you, Michael, just who are you?"

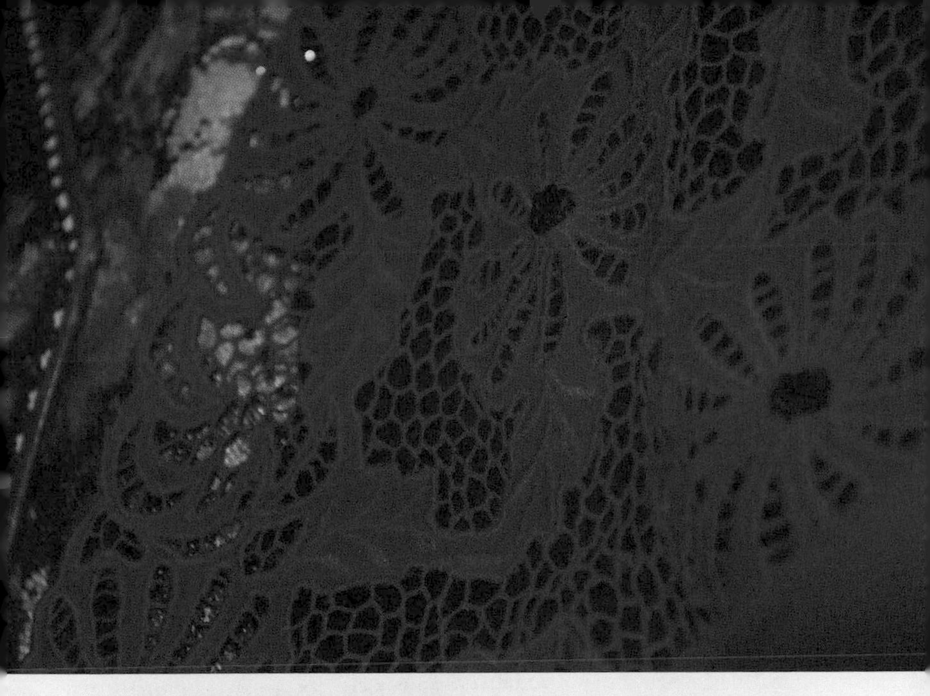

Detail of one of my early kebayas made specially for me when I was in my early 20s. My mother brought me to a kebaya maker's shop at the Central Market in Kuala Lumpur and encouraged me to choose my own design. I chose a red Swiss cotton material and a chrysanthemum and honeycomb motif embroidered in red and black.

My parents, sister (bottom right) and me. My Papa insisted that as nyonyas, we should learn to wear a kebaya. He took the family to Penang on a holiday when I was twelve, and my sister and I had our very first kebayas made. Mine was a light yellow kebaya biku *and hers a pink one.*

A family trip back to Malacca to visit Chimpo (Grandaunt) and Chek Kong (Granduncle) at their home near Bukit China, 1968. I am on the left in a kebaya. With me are my mother, sister and brother.

The Wedding Photo

I had always felt that I didn't quite belong, I don't know why. I somehow never felt quite part of my family. For one thing, I don't look like my sister and brother at all. I am the oldest daughter. After me comes my younger sister, Gek Bee, and my brother, Teck Beng. Both Gek Bee and Beng have small close-set eyes, just like my father's and his fine thin hair. But I have big eyes and look quite different from them. They are both fair just like my parents but I am dusky in complexion.

I often thought about it when I was very young but at that time, I couldn't quite put a finger on the problem. I just felt different. It wasn't that my Mother and Father didn't love me. In fact, they were good to me. Father was quite distant from me, though. He would hug my sister and brother but he never once hugged nor kissed me. Mother was always kind and caring, though sometimes she was very strict, especially with me.

And then of course, there was that odd thing about my surname. My brother and sister are both Chongs, like my parents. But my surname is Tan.

"Why is my surname different from the rest of you all?" I asked my mother when I was seven years old.

"Oh, that's because we fished you out from the sea," Mother smiled and then dismissed me quickly.

They always made up all kinds of stories in answer to my question – Mother, Grandma, my aunts...stories such as a stork brought me into the house one day, or I was found discarded by the roadside, or I was picked up from a dustbin.

I thought nothing of it until one day, I asked my mother again.

A frown appeared on her face.

"Okay, now listen carefully and don't ask me again anymore after this. You were the firstborn and you were a girl. The other side didn't like it so they said, no she should not be called a Chong, she will just have to follow the mother's surname. So you were called Tan which is my maiden surname. That's why your name appears as Tan Gek Kim on the birth certificate, when it should be Chong Gek Kim. Okay? Now no more silly questions."

That was the reason I settled for. I believed what she told me. Just like that. Well, I was just seven then. I wasn't even sure what a birth certificate was.

But as the Chinese say, paper cannot cover fire and it got worse as I grew older. When I went to school and had to fill in forms and things like that, the children in school started to tease me. They started calling me bastard.

"Bastard! Bastard! Gek Kim is a bastard!" some of the schoolchildren would chant.

"Stop it! Stop it! Stop calling me names," I screamed at them.

On my tenth birthday, my aunt, Mother's third sister

came all the way down from Penang to Ipoh to visit me. I liked her a lot.

My aunt was the most beautiful of the seven sisters, I thought. She had an oval-shaped face, was *hitam manis* in complexion and was always graceful in her movements and demeanour. I called her Second Aunt. She was my favourite aunt but I only got to see her a few times a year mainly at family reunions or during Chinese New Year.

"Happy birthday, Gek Kim. I have a present for you," she said gently as she knelt down beside me and handed me a beautifully wrapped package.

She was the only one of my many aunts and uncles who remembered my birthday and always sent me a present.

"Go on, don't be shy. Open it," she urged when she saw me hesitantly holding the parcel.

I tore open the present excitedly with all the impatience of a happy ten-year-old. I gasped with delight. It was a lovely silk dress with fine lace at the edges and a red sash. It was gorgeous and it looked really expensive. I had never owned anything that beautiful in my life.

"Thank you, Second Aunty," I said shyly.

She stroked my hair gently and murmured, "My, you are growing up so quickly."

I looked up at her and was surprised to see tears in her eyes.

I wondered why Second Aunt was sad. Had I said something to make her unhappy? Or maybe she was just happy that I was growing up, I thought innocently.

Impulsively, I hugged her. I loved the fragrance of her. She smelt like fresh flowers on a dewy morning. She smelt familiar, a soft lovely scent that I could vaguely remember from my childhood. She was always dressed elegantly in beautiful *cheongsams* which showed off her slim, shapely figure. She hugged me tightly in return. Then, she suddenly pulled herself away from me and said, "I've got to go."

She left abruptly. She looked quite upset.

She was still single, and for as long as I could remember she had always been alone – no husband, no boyfriend.

Later, I asked my mother about Second Aunt.

"Why doesn't Second Aunt have a husband? Why is Second Aunt always alone?"

Mother looked startled. She seemed disturbed by my questions.

"Oh, Second Aunt did have somebody once. But it was an unhappy love affair."

"Oh," I said, "What do you mean?"

"Second Aunt was once in love with a married man. He was crazy about her. He wanted to leave his wife and children for her. She refused. She wanted to end it, but he refused to give up on her."

"What happened? Did she marry him?"

"No. He already had a family. She could not bring herself to break up his family. So she ran away to Penang and cut off all contact with him. She's always been alone since. I think she never quite got over him."

I didn't understand. I shrugged and after a while,

forgot all about Second Aunt.

I was still getting taunted in school. A number of girls in my class just would not let up on the bullying and teasing.

"Bastard, bastard! Tan Gek Kim is a bastard."

"Gek Kim, Gek Kim. Come from the dustbin!"

I was sickened by their mindless taunts. How much more did I have to suffer this cruelty? One day, I went up to one of my tormentors and slapped her on the face. I was punished severely by the teacher and made to stand in the hot sun for half an hour.

When I came home, I burst into tears in front of my mother.

"They are spreading lies about me, Mother, horrible lies," I cried. "I can't take it anymore."

But Mother just kept quiet.

"Do something, Mother. Why can't you do something? Make them stop calling me these horrible names."

I could not understand why Mother was not angry. She didn't even appear indignant.

She sighed and said, "Don't bother about them. Just ignore them."

A few weeks later, my parents had to travel out of town for a few days to visit a sick relative. Uncle Mickey, Mother's youngest brother, came over to take care of us. He was on a long semester break from university.

That evening, I decided to put on the beautiful dress Second Aunt had given me. I ran to my parents' bedroom to look at the mirror.

I got distracted by the things on Mother's dressing table. She had all sorts of interesting bottles of perfume and little pots of lotions and powder, lipsticks and jewellery.

I was sitting at the dressing table, playing happily with Mother's cosmetics, when from the corner of my eye, something caught my attention. It was an old photo album sticking out from under the bed. I had never seen it before. Why was it under the bed?

I pulled it out. They were photos of my parents' wedding. A photo fell out. I picked it up and stared at it.

Horror! Horror! I felt like dying. I couldn't breathe. I gasped and gagged.

The photo was a beautiful wedding photo – of a beaming wedding couple with their family all around them, posing happily for the camera. But I had never felt so wretched in my life.

For there I was! In that photograph! I was sitting on my Mother's lap. How could that be? My parents were just getting married. This was their wedding day! How could I be in the photo? I couldn't have been born yet. I knew vaguely that people only make babies after they get married. Something was terribly wrong.

I looked about two years old in that photo – I could recognise myself from my other baby photos in Mother's photo albums. I was perched on my mother's lap. Someone else in the photo had an arm placed gently on my shoulder, helping Mother to balance me on her lap amidst the folds of her white wedding dress. I peered incredulously at the photo and recognised her as Second Aunt.

Suddenly the memory of Second Aunt's tears at my tenth birthday came to mind. I thought about how she never forgot my birthday, her special affection for me, my odd surname, my surname which was different from my family's but was the same surname as Second Aunt's. I wanted to blot out the thoughts that were surfacing in my head.

Things were slowly beginning to make sense.

The lies, the lies...they were beginning to turn into truths, lies that had hurt me were turning into truths that hurt even more.

I ran to find Uncle Mickey. I screamed, "Uncle Mickey, Uncle Mickey!"

He was watching television in the living room downstairs.

"Tell me," I sobbed, "What is the meaning of this? Why am I in here, in my parents' wedding photo?"

Uncle Mickey was startled. He didn't quite know what to say at first. After much pleading, he told me the truth.

"Look, Kim, you'd better not tell your parents I told you this, okay? They'll kill me. I know you won't leave me alone otherwise, so I might as well come out with it," he muttered.

"Well...it's like this. Actually your parents aren't your parents. Your mother isn't your mother. Second Aunt is your real mother. And your mother is actually your Third Aunt," he said.

I felt as if my blood was being drained away from me.

"Second Aunt gave birth to you out of wedlock," he continued.

"What's that?" I asked.

"That means she wasn't married when she gave birth to you. You are an illegitimate child," he said.

"She brought you up for the first two years all by herself. It was a big scandal, I remember. There was so much nasty gossip and talking behind our backs," he continued.

"Then when Third Sister – er that would be your 'Mother' – got married, the family decided this was the chance to stop all the gossip. Second Aunt was pressured by everyone in the family, especially by her parents, to give you up to your 'Mother'.

"Oh," I said bravely. I was just ten years old and it was hard to know even what to say.

Uncle Mickey went on. "Chong, your Mother's husband-to-be, was quite reluctant at first about this arrangement, but finally was persuaded to adopt you as his daughter. You were around two years old by then when you were adopted."

"And what about my real father? Who is he?"

"I don't know. I heard he killed himself or something like that when Second Aunt rejected him."

All this took place a long time ago when I was just ten years old. I harbour no bitterness towards anyone. I am a successful businesswoman today. I don't keep in touch very much with the family anymore. Only sometimes, at the occasional family gathering or the Chinese New Year Eve dinner.

It is my birthday today. I am forty-five years old today. I went into town and bought myself a beautiful dress, the same colour as the one I had on my tenth birthday. It was terribly expensive too, but I didn't care. Like Second Aunt, I don't have a husband nor a boyfriend. I don't need love. In fact, I don't want to love — then, I won't ever get hurt.

I don't need anyone. I just want to keep my life as simple and uncomplicated as possible.

No messiness, that's all.

Ayam berkokok hari nak siang
Murai bunyi pada pagi
Sedeh hati kaseh nak pulang
Bila kah bolih berjumpa lagi?

The rooster crows at the break of dawn
The magpie sings in the early morn
My sad lovelorn heart yearns to return
When can we meet again?

A baba *pantun*

The nyonyas loved to match their sarong kebayas with beaded shoes known as kasut manik. *The beads came from countries such as the former Czechoslovakia, Austria and Germany.*

Marry Me, Marianne

The journey started on a perfect note. When he went to pick her up from her home in Petaling Jaya on an early Sunday morning, the hummingbirds were busy siphoning nectar from the huge red hibiscus flowers, birds were chirping after a rainwashed night, a pair of squirrels dashed cheerily up and down the mango tree in the garden.

Marianne's fat ginger tabby stretched out luxuriously on the frazzled wicker chair, fluffed itself a few times then jumped down to greet Peter, rubbing herself sensually against his left leg. Marianne appeared at the door, eyes dancing with excitement, smiling a little shyly. Peter took her Overnighter duffel bag from her, stood there for a moment looking at her lovingly.

Holding hands, they strolled to Peter's car, blissfully happy. Today was the day – the day when they would make the two-hour journey to Peter's parents' home in Ipoh to meet his folks. Peter drove through the streets of the older section of Petaling Jaya town, still quiet and slumbering on a Sunday morning, and headed for the highway to Ipoh.

"This is it, Marianne," he said excitedly, "I can't wait for my parents to meet you. I know they will love you. You will like my Pa – he is a real lady-killer. He can charm the birds down from the trees."

Peter had met Marianne at a friend's engagement party five months ago and they were attracted to each other instantly. They went out a few times and somewhere along the way, fell in love with each other. He felt very sure she was the one – this lovely, exciting woman by his side – the one he wanted to spend the rest of his life with. He had been badly burnt in a previous relationship, enough to scare him off women for quite awhile. The incessant demands, the jealousy, the quarrels and the accusations were hard to take. It ended badly, full of bitter words when once they were tender with love and admiration.

Then, along came Marianne. Intelligent, enchanting Marianne. Funny, laidback yet passionate about life, she was a joy to be with. He loved her sense of humour, her spontaneity. Peter felt a wonderful sense of ease when he was with her, a feeling of lightness. There was this connection that didn't require words – they could sense each other's moods, understand keenly what the other was feeling.

Marianne smiled, a little nervous at the thought of meeting her future in-laws for the first time, "I'm sure they are two wonderful perfectly normal people. I don't know how on earth they produced someone as crazy as you though," she teased.

He laughed, "Takes one to know one."

He leaned over and gave her a gentle kiss on her cheek. He noticed a faint blush under her fair complexion. She reached out for his hand, held it for a few moments. Her eyes said it all, full of love and tenderness for him.

As he wove his car out of the early morning tangle of traffic and swung onto the northbound highway, he stole a glance at her again. She was dressed in a casual light blue top, and her hair, always gorgeously unruly with a life of its own, was reined in at the nape of her neck with a large butterfly-shaped clip. She had the kind of looks that made people stop and stare whenever she entered a room, but she seemed blithely unaware. He felt his heart would burst. Throughout the journey to Ipoh, they talked of their future together.

"I'll sell off my bachelor's apartment and buy a house with some land in the suburbs. How about that, Marianne?"

"It'll be nice to have a garden. But I don't really care as long as I can be with you."

"And we'll have six kids, what do you think?"

"What? Six? Are you nuts? Two's fine, a boy and a girl. Perfect."

Nothing untoward happened along the way, but a hint of something vaguely disconcerting emerged, only to be lightly brushed away.

"Strange that I'm from Ipoh too but we never met," Marianne piped up after they'd passed the Tapah rest stop along the highway.

"Yeah, but Ipoh's got a huge population. You can't possibly meet everyone from the same hometown."

"I feel as if I've known you for a long time, Peter, even though it's been only five months since we first met."

"I know what you mean. There's this strange connection...I don't know how to explain it."

"Maybe we met in an earlier life, maybe we were best friends or lovers in a previous life."

"Aww, don't give me this previous life nonsense," Peter groaned.

"How'd you know? Maybe I was an Egyptian princess in an earlier life."

"Yeah right, and I was Mark Anthony."

They laughed and Marianne gave him a playful pinch.

"Owww that hurts," Peter pretended to flinch in agony.

"I still think I have met you before, somewhere a long time ago but I just can't figure out where or when," Marianne said nonchalantly.

The journey was pleasant, full of promise, until they reached Ipoh. Peter skillfully navigated his way through Ipoh town, and finally, on to Gilmore Road, the road leading to an older suburb where his parents lived.

It was then he noticed Marianne getting visibly nervous. A frown hovered tentatively on her brow where she had been glowing with happiness earlier.

"What's wrong, Marianne?"

"What do you mean what's wrong?"

"Well, you look worried. Relax, my parents won't eat you. I know they will adore you, the way I do."

He reached out for her hand and pressed it to his lips.

She pulled away nervously; it was something she had never done before.

"Are you sure you are taking me to visit your parents? Are you sure this is where they live?"

"But of course. I grew up here, in this part of town. This is where I spent much of my childhood before Pa sent me to do my O-levels in England."

She didn't respond, just sat there quietly, scrutinising the surroundings.

Peter noticed her mounting unease.

"Is there a problem? Marianne, if you don't feel up to it, we don't have to do this. We can always meet them some other time. It's just that I want them to meet you. My Pa will be smitten by you. Pa loves beautiful women, I'll have to take care he doesn't steal you from me," he teased.

In a very soft voice, she answered, "So does my Pa."

"Does he?" Peter laughed, "Well, I guess they have something in common. But then, which man doesn't?"

"Doesn't what?" Marianne echoed, her attention focused on the passing scenery of old government bungalows gracefully laid out in spacious compounds, bordered by fences overgrown with rambling Honolulu creepers and purple morning glory. Orange and bright red bougainvillea tumbled out of slightly wild, unkept gardens and at one junction, the stately flame-of-the-forest tree clothed the grass with clusters of spent flowers, still blazing red in a dying splendour.

"Doesn't love beauti..." his voice trailed away as he

caught sight of her ashen face.

"What's wrong, Marianne? You've turned completely pale."

Her face seemed to be drained of blood as Peter manoeuvered the last few corners of the narrow roads. Every corner brought to her expressive face a mounting tension. Her left hand playing nervously before with the loose strands of her hair, now clutched at her heart.

She looked like a trapped animal. Her anxiety unnerved Peter. It was something bigger, he knew, than just a young woman going to meet her future in-laws.

"If you like, we can turn back, Marianne," he tried to say calmly.

"No," snapped Marianne. "Drive on. We've got to resolve this."

"Resolve what? If you don't want to meet my folks, that's fine. And if you are not ready for marriage, if you have changed your mind, that's okay too. I understand. I will be a sorry mess but I will wait for you. I love you, Marianne, more than words can ever express, more than anything in the world."

Something in her glazed expression egged him on now. She stared straight ahead, the frightened look in her eyes told him he had to reach that destination. The answer lay there, he knew, though he knew not what.

She was silent, her hands lying quietly in her lap. There was no more room for words. No more time to learn more about each other. He began to regret that he had rushed the courtship.

Then she said something that made him laugh with relief.

"We never quite talked about our childhood. We never took the time to compare notes about our families. We shouldn't have rushed, Peter. We...we don't even know the names of each other's parents."

"Is that it then, Marianne? Is there something about your parents you want to tell me? I don't care what or who they are. I know they must be pretty special to have brought up someone like you."

Peter turned the last corner, drove up a sharp incline into a large compound.

He gasped, "Wow, look, the traveller's palm has gotten so huge."

Marianne replied quietly, "Yes, it has, hasn't it?"

Peter turned and looked at her. A terrible lump of fear was shaping inside him, writhing in horror...

"Marianne, now that you mention it...I'd better tell you that my Pa has seven wives. I didn't think it would matter at all, I thought I'd tell you in time to come. I am the son of his second wife. He lives here with her. His other wives are all living on their own and he sort of moves around from wife to wife. But he is a great dad and I know you will like him and not hold this against him, nor me...but...what about you? You said you are from Ipoh too...who are...who are you?" Peter blurted out at breakneck speed, grasping for a lifeline, bidding for time against the darkness swirling in his head, a truth too frightening to face.

There was only a deathly silence.

Then she piped up, her voice aching with pain, "My Mum is a single mother. She separated from my father a long time ago when I was eight. She got fed up with his polygamous lifestyle. I think she was the fifth or sixth wife, she wouldn't say. I've not seen my father for a long time. He brought me here when I was very young, a few times to play in this garden. That's why everything seems vaguely familiar."

Peter could not bear to look at Marianne. He looked out of the window, at the pink hibiscus studding the thick hedges, nodding in the light morning breeze, at the spider orchids clinging to his favourite rambutan tree, at the traveller's palm, only a small sapling when his father had planted it on his seventh birthday, now grown into a giant fan, its thick green leaves paddling the air.

He stepped out of the car and pressed his head against the roof of the car, closing his eyes shut, trying to steady himself. Then he bent down to look at Marianne one more time, and looked at her the way a man looks at a woman he loves.

She was unreachable now, shut away in a faraway place; only the tears streaming down her face belied her devastation. She sat frozen, staring straight ahead, her heart breaking along, she knew, with his. Her eyes refused to meet his.

An elderly man stepped out of the house, and came

towards them, his face lit up on seeing his son. He was still handsome for someone in his seventies, silver hair framing a swarthy charming face, his frame still athletic for his age, though he hobbled a little from a bad knee.

"Peter, welcome home. Sylvia, come on out into the garden, Pete's back!" he yelled for his wife, "Now Peter, where is your beautiful young fiancé that you have been telling us so much about? We are looking forward to meeting your future wife."

"Peter? What's wrong?"

A slim, beautiful woman stepped out of the car. The old man stepped back in shock and disbelief. She looked the spitting image of Wife Number Five, Ai Ling.

Marianne stepped out of the car, brushing at her tears.

"Hi Pa," she said.

HOW TO BE A GOOD DAUGHTER-IN-LAW

Teik gar kee, moh hor chee,
Cho lung sim poo, but toh lee:
Um um khoon, char char khee,
Say thow, buat hoon, tiam eng chee;
Jip pung lye, gim chiam chee,
Jip tua thniah, cheng toke ee,
Jip chow khar, say uah tee;
Oh loh hiah, oh loh tee,
Oh loh chin keh chen mm gow kar see.

Dried bean curd, sweetened buns,
To be a good daughter-in-law, know your manners:
Go to bed late, get up early,
Comb your hair, powder your face, dab on rouge,
Enter a room holding a needle,
Go to the main hall and wash the crockery;
Praise your elder and younger brothers-in-law,
Your parents in turn will be praised for
your good upbringing.

Hokkien ditty from Yeap Joo Kim, 1992.
"Of Comb, Powder and Rouge"
(Singapore: Lee Teng Lay Pte Ltd, 35-6)

Beaded clutch purses in vibrant colours with motifs of dragons, bats and phoenixes from Chinese mythology and English country gardens, and dainty silver mesh bags were favoured by the nyonyas to complement the sarong kebaya ensemble. (Beaded purses courtesy Dr. Harriet Wong)

The nyonyas wore belts of silver to secure their sarongs. The belt above was given to me by my mother and is made up of hundreds of linked and decorated silver chains. The motifs on the buckles of these silver belts ranged from flowers, leaves, birds and animals to human figures.

The Courtesan from Gion

"You are Japanese! Admit it! You stupid bitch," he screams at her.

"I am not Japanese. I am Straits Chinese," she replies calmly.

"Confess, woman. You are Yuki, the courtesan. Confess now or you will surely die. Enough of this ridiculous pretense."

"I am Jade, the wife of Baba Robert Tan. I have lived all my life in Tengkera. Now let me go."

"And you speak Japanese – how is that possible?"

"My neighbour was a Japanese. I learnt how to speak Japanese from him."

"My my, he must have been a very good teacher."

With one swift movement, he slaps her hard across her right cheek.

"Liar! Do you think I'm stupid?"

She gasps as her head spins, electric stars bursting in her head.

He approaches her again, his face contorted in an ugly sneer. He thrusts his thick clumsy hand into the front of her white cotton blouse. The buttons snap and fall on the cold cement floor as he tears at her blouse.

He taunts, "Your skin looks Japanese. And your body sure looks Japanese to me."

The two soldiers holding her on each side smirk and chortle, while Yashimaya, from the dreaded Kempetai continues interrogating her.

"Now will you confess or do I need to conduct further investigation?"

"Take your filthy hands off me. I am just a simple woman. I have not committed any crime against the Japanese. Let me go."

"Not committed any crime? You have committed the biggest crime of all – denouncing your Japanese identity. We are the victors in this war. We have triumphed beyond our wildest dreams. And yet you, you traitor, you dare denounce your origins. You dare betray our cause."

He continues ranting at her. "You were brought over here to spy on the British. You were not supposed to join them. I'm giving you one last chance – if you admit you are Yuki, we welcome you back. We need pleasure workers like you to spy on our enemies. If you don't, you will be executed for treason."

"You've got the wrong person."

He grabs her hair from behind and yanks her head backwards. Bringing his face to within inches of hers, he snarls menacingly.

"We know you are her. You are Yuki-*san*, the talented courtesan gone missing. We have been searching for you for a long time, Yuki. Now confess."

She can see the insides of his mouth, the lead fillings in his molars, the chipped enamel of his front tooth, the pinkish slobbery tongue. She struggles but he holds her hair in an iron grip. The stale smell of whisky and cigarettes from his spittle-frothing mouth nauseates her.

She summons all her strength and spits at him.

"I'm Jade, Nyonya Jade Tan Swee Neo from Tengkera. Please remove your slimy face away from mine."

He springs back in shock, wiping the sputum off his face, then explodes in anger and rains blows on her. He yells at the guards, "Take her away. At dawn tomorrow, you will be executed."

Yashimaya warns grimly, "That is all, Yuki. I have given you every chance but you have turned them all down. I cannot save you now."

He watches her intently hoping that she understands, but she gives no signs at all.

He pounds his fist on the table as the guards drag her out, furious that he could not make her confess to her true identity. He is used to winning in everything but this pale, delicate woman is tougher than he previously thought.

He screams at her as she is dragged out half-conscious, "One last chance. I give you one more chance. Because you are Japanese. If you confess tomorrow morning, your life will be spared. If not, you will be beheaded."

Jade is thrown into her cell, in the basement of a school converted into a Kempetai interrogation centre. There is no window, just a sliver of light through a crack in the wall. The cell is cold and damp, cockroaches scurry about, antennae twitching defiantly, surprised at having to share their space with an intruder. The smell of excrement and stale urine is nauseating. Dark furry things brush against her feet.

Her stomach lurches every time shrieks and howls of agony penetrate the air through the thick cold walls. She claps her hands tightly over her ears, trying to shut out the blood-chilling screams. She shudders. She is glad her interrogation is over. Tomorrow is the day of reckoning for her. She cannot bear it any more – the daily assaults, the verbal and physical abuse, her abject humiliation.

They try to break me, every day they use their brutality to try and break my spirit, my mind. Yet they dare not scar me, they want me with my body intact to lure men, to spy for them. I will never agree.

I was a courtesan in Gion, Kyoto...but that was a long time ago...almost ten, or was it twelve years ago? I was young, innocent, just a maiko, *learning to become a geisha. I sang, danced, played the shamisen, learnt the fine arts of the geisha. But I was tricked by a rich patron who persuaded me to come over to Malaya with him. He had a thriving business empire over here, he told me. He promised me a life of luxury in a tropical paradise. I was so naïve and I suppose, a little in love with him. But the reality was he tricked me. Once I came over, he forced me to be part of an espionage ring in British Malaya. With no money and nowhere to go, I was forced to spy on the British and the locals. I learnt that the Japanese were planning an invasion of the Malay peninsula, they needed to gather as much information as possible. Who better than the courtesan, the barber, the masseuse, people you are relaxed with, let down your guard with.*

I did not sleep with men when I was a maiko *in Gion. Geishas are skilled courtesans, ladies of the night, but these fools have gotten us wrong — we entertain, we titillate, we pleasure but we do not engage in deceit and espionage. I was trained to give, not to extract. Oh what a terrible life I had here. I was miserable, I hated it, I could not bear the deception, the pretense, I could not bear having to sell myself for a cause I didn't even believe in. I longed to return to Japan, to the lovely fragile world of the Floating City, but I could not bear the shame. I wanted to die, kill myself.*

One night, I tried. I escaped from the watchful eyes of my abductors, made my way to the river and threw myself in. The currents were strong, I could not swim and felt myself being pulled down under. Aahhh, I was happy to succumb, anything to end my wretched life, but someone came along. A gentleman pulled me out. I screamed at him to let me die, but he wouldn't let go. My rescuer brought me back to his home — a strange, long, house that never seemed to end. I was shivering, more dead than alive, pleading for death.

His mother took pity on me. Why do you want to die? Life is too beautiful to shorten too soon, she told me. At that time, I couldn't comprehend her. I could not understand the strange language she spoke in. It sounded like a Malay dialect to me, but it had many other languages, all mixed up in it. She told her son they should take me in, she was sure I'd kill myself again if I was left on my own.

They gave me a place to stay, they took care of me. They sensed I was in some kind of trouble and gave me shelter. I was terrified that the Japanese syndicate would find me, drag me back into that horrible life I abhorred, but this kind family protected me. The gentleman who rescued me was Robert Tan. His wife had passed away a few years ago. I was young then, still attractive — he must have taken a liking to me. I became his wife eventually.

They gave me a name, helped me to 'disappear'. I was called Jade. No one was allowed to call me Yuki. Yuki the Japanese courtesan disappeared, and in her place, I became Jade, the Nyonya from Tengkera.

I learnt that I had been rescued and taken in by a Chinese family in Malacca. Chinese and yet not completely one hundred per cent Chinese. They called themselves Straits Chinese, baba for the men and nyonya for the women folk. To become one of them, I had to learn their ways. I enjoyed becoming a nyonya, although there were many nights I cried silently, secretly, unable to understand what they were speaking, unable to eat their hot spicy food. Changing my identity wasn't instant, I had to learn many things — how to speak their language, dress like them, eat with my fingers, behave like them, learn their customs and rituals. My mother-in-law, Bibik Chim was an excellent teacher.

It's not so different, really, from my life in Gion.

Instead of wearing a kimono, I had to learn how to wear a sarong and the beautiful voile blouse called kebaya — it's hard work. One has to practise and practise in order to pin the kerosang *correctly. The* kerosang *has three brooches linked with a delicate chain and I feared that I would make big holes in my kebaya. And the kebaya must hug the body just nicely with both sides exactly symmetrical. Its two tails must point out at exact and similar angles. The sarong must wrap around gracefully, not flaring out like a tent. I had to learn not to take mincing steps like a geisha, but to walk with a gentle sway of the hips, like a nyonya.*

Always walk slowly and gracefully. Don't run, Bibik Chim says. A nyonya looks ridiculous if she takes big manly strides and her sarong will flap and create a wind. Speak softly, a loud woman is crass and ugly. Bibik Chim always spoke in the gentlest of tones but everyone respected her.

Nyonyas are always seronoh, *Bibik says.* Seronoh *was her favourite word. Everything must be seronoh, which means to be refined and graceful.*

Be well-groomed always, Bibik Chim told me. That wasn't difficult as I had learnt the importance of good grooming in Gion. But I learnt to adorn myself with tropical flowers such as jasmine and orchids in my hair and jewellery which Robert gave me on my ears and neck and wrists.

Respect your elders. Never forget your ancestors. They are our link to our past. Worship them by offering prayers in their memory, piara abu, take care of their cremated ashes, Mother-in-law Bibik Chim taught me. I have no ancestors I know of, my parents were killed in a terrible earthquake in Kyoto when I was just six years old and I was given away by a distant aunt to be trained as a maiko *in Gion. I do not know who my ancestors in Japan are. I only have a faint memory of my parents. I regard Robert's family as mine. I finally have a family, and a future if not a past. Every evening, I offered prayers at the family altar, and on special occasions helped prepare fabulous feasts in memory of our ancestors.*

Learn how to cook. The secret in pleasuring a man is not just in the bedroom, but also in the kitchen, Bibik says, winking and chuckling. Wonderful food, presented beautifully, is as tempting and as seductive as a woman beckoning with her body. The way to a man's heart is through the stomach, she declared though she thinks that comes from an English proverb, not from the nyonyas. I learnt quickly, desperate to shed whatever Japanese-ness I had that would bring attention to me. They never found me. To everyone, I was Jade, a distant niece of Bibik who became Mrs Robert Tan. My abductors could not comprehend how Yuki just vanished into thin air. I mastered the language really fast too. When you are desperate, you learn fast.

Then in 1941, the Japanese swept through Malaya on their bicycles, conquered it swiftly and ruled it with terrible oppression. But still, for a while, my world was untroubled and peaceful. I was blessed with a beautiful baby boy, my darling son, Kenny, my baby, someone who truly belongs to me. I was so happy and content, I had a home and a family and respect from everyone. I was a good person with nothing to be ashamed of. Life was good.

Until they came and took me away. Someone, perhaps someone who knew me from my past, betrayed me to the Japanese.

She hears loud footsteps stomping down the corridor. A greasy enamel bowl of watery rice with some green bits floating in it is thrust under her door.

"If I am to die tomorrow, can't I have better food?" she asks.

"Hah! Don't kid yourself. You won't die, you'll live. You are Japanese, remember? You'll choose the right thing, then you can eat to your heart's content with all the men you have to sleep with," jeers the guard.

She looks at her torn clothes, the welts, ugly bruises and dried blood stains on her arms and legs. Her body is battered and bruised, she hasn't bathed and washed for days. She remembers Bibik Chim's words...

Put bedak sejuk *every day on your face to keep it cool and smooth, scent your clothes with potpourris of* bunga rampei, *wear diamonds and* intan *on your ears.*

Make your house a home. Be happy. 'Smile and the whole world smiles with you, weep and you weep alone', although that too, she thinks, is an English proverb.

She can hear Bibik Chim's gentle jovial voice, floating all around her.

Jade breaks down and weeps.

The next morning, she is awakened by the cocks' crowing. She knows it is only a matter of time now before they come for her. She has to decide what to do.

If I choose life, then I can go home and cuddle my baby, hold him close and never let him go. I can be Jade again, cook my favourite dishes, ayam pong teh *and* babi buah keluak, *eat my favourite nyonya cakes, walk along the streets of Malacca without fear, ride the trishaw to the market to buy my* sireh *and fresh* santan, *take care of my child and my husband and Bibik, love them the way they have loved me. I owe them my life...but no, I am just fooling myself.*

The truth is, if I choose life, I have to denounce my nyonya identity, switch over to their side, be a spy for them, never ever see my baby and my family again, leave them for good, renounce everything I have grown to love and cherish, become a spy and a slut for them. How can I bear it? I want my son to remember me as a good, honest person, respected by society. A good mother, the wife of Mr Robert Tan. My son must never know my past. I want him to grow up, hold his head high and be able to say to everyone, My Mama was a good person. Don't ever insult her memory.

I must choose. I must.

If I choose life, then I still have breath in my body even though I am dead inside with sadness, heartbreak...just to be able to see a garden dripping with dew in the early morning, to see a leaf twirl its way gently down in a breeze, to dance to my favourite tune, to hear the haunting notes of the shamisen, to watch the sun set over the Straits of Malacca, to just be alive.

There were noises in the corridor. Loud yells, tramping of boots and clanging of keys. Her door is thrown open. The guards haul her up roughly from the plank bed and drag her up the stairs and out into the courtyard. There, they force her to kneel in the sunshine, with her hands tied behind her back.

Yashimaya, standing in the shadows behind a pillar, emerges, stubbing out a cigarette, an ingratiating, half-mocking grin on his face.

"I gather you have good news for me, Yuki-*san*."

She remains silent.

A tiny bluish vein begins to throb on the left side of Yashimaya's forehead.

"Now don't play games with me. It's taken far too long. Remember what I said, if you confess you live. If you don't, you die."

A burly Japanese guard, dressed in long loose black pants positions himself next to her, holding a Samurai sword in his hands. He brings the sword slowly down and places it on her neck. She jolts in shock when she feels the cold hard steel. She cannot stop shaking, tears stream down her face. She wants to live more than anything – she has no causes, no ideology, no battles to fight. She keeps the image of her son in her mind, focusing singularly on him, trying to blot everything else out.

Yashimaya barks, "Now what do you choose? Are you Yuki-*san* or not? Do you choose Life? Or Death?"

She shouts, "I choose Love and Honour and Respect. I am Jade, not Yuki and be damned with you."

Yashimaya swears and spits on the floor. He gestures with his hands.

The executioner lifts the sword up high over Jade. It glints in the sunshine, poised for an eternity, then it comes down swiftly through her stark white neck.

The nyonya kebaya is the modern and more fashionable version of the baju panjang *worn by the nyonyas in the past. The* baju panjang *or* 'th'ng sah' *(long dress in Hokkien) was a loose top, usually stiffly starched, fastened by a* kerosang *worn over a cotton batik sarong.*

From the 1920s, the baju panjang *was eventually replaced by the modern nyonya kebaya, a more shapely, feminine and sensual garment with delicate embroidery at the neckline, sleeves and hem.*

(above) Close-up of three baju panjang *made from German organdie; (left) my collection of* baju panjang *which belonged to my maternal grandmother, Teh Swee Neo.*

My mother, Kwee Hoon, at her wedding, with her mother, Teh Swee Neo seated behind her. My maternal grandmother (above right) lived just long enough to see her eldest daughter marry before she succumbed to cancer in 1946. A Penang nyonya, she had seven daughters and two sons. Educated to Form Five level, she believed passionately in education for her daughters. A strong matriach figure, she survived the Japanese Occupation by making nyonya kueh to sell. Her daughters had to be hidden away in the countryside far from harm during the Occupation, while her two young sons sold nyonya kueh, *peddling the precious cakes on a rickety old bicycle.*

Wedding photo of my maternal grandmother in a baju panjang *and her husband, Foo Ah Poe.*

A Promise is a Promise

"Promise me, Bebe, if it is a girl, you will give her to me. Promise?" Sue Kwan begged.

Bebe, six months pregnant, hesitated. She looked at her cousin Sue Kwan, pale, uptight and pleading, sadness in her eyes. After ten years of a childless marriage, Sue Kwan was desperate. Bebe was desperate too – for a son. She already had three daughters.

Bebe knew her husband and entire clan would be disappointed if her baby turned out to be a girl. It had been one pregnancy after another ever since she got married. If she could only have a son, her husband would stop pestering her to keep trying. A son would ensure the continuity of the family line, an heir at last to inherit the vast family fortunes. And remove the excuse for her husband to take another wife or a concubine. She was weary of being pregnant, her body was feeling the strain. A son would put an end to all these long, uncomfortable pregnancy interludes.

She was startled to see Sue Kwan on her knees.

"Please, Bebe, please. Promise me."

"Oh Sue Kwan, don't do that," Bebe, embarrassed, gently pulled Sue Kwan up. Sue Kwan wouldn't stop.

"If it's a daughter, give her to me. You already have three. What is another to you? But she will be everything to me. I will love her like my own. Do you promise?"

"Okay, I promise," Bebe mouthed softly, gave her cousin a reassuring squeeze on her arm.

Why on earth did I do that? Bebe thought after Sue Kwan had left, chauffeured in her plush sedan back to her grand mansion along the Esplanade. She felt pity for her cousin. She used to be a vivacious girl, full of fun and spontaneity. She seemed to have shrivelled up inside after her marriage to a businessman from one of the wealthiest Baba families in Malacca. She was in love with someone else, it was whispered, but he was of Portuguese descent, a comprador working for her father – an unsuitable match, they said. Her parents hastily married her off to a distant cousin, twelve years her senior. It was a lonely marriage, worsened by barrenness, the blame placed entirely on Sue Kwan.

"Boy or girl?" Bebe stroked the gentle swell of her belly, pondering over her unborn child.

Ah Sum, her Cantonese *amah* and house cook, predicted it would be a boy.

"Chinese people always say, mother's stomach pointed and mother looking good, then surely Boy. Mother's stomach round and mother looking ugly, untidy, then surely Girl. You, Ah Tai Soh, very neat-looking, stomach pointed. For sure, you getting Boy!"

Bebe looked into the mirror of the mahogany sideboard, an ornate furniture piece with an Italian marble top, decorative mini spires and carvings of flowers. A lovely young woman with a high forehead and high cheekbones stared back at her. The slight rise of her stomach was just discernible under her light green kebaya.

During Sue Kwan's ride home in her husband's newly-acquired 1927 sedan, she had an anxiety attack again, torn between elation and despair. What if Bebe agreed to give her the baby girl? Why, she would have a child at last. Someone to love with all her heart and soul, to shower all her maternal instincts upon. She had longed for a child for years but every month, her period arrived right on the dot, taunting her with its annoying regularity. Her husband had not bedded her very much too, the tension and pressure doused whatever little passion he had for her.

Mother-in-law's whispers behind her back graduated from snide remarks about barren women to open displays of temper. The many servant girls in the opulent household where Sue Kwan lived got the brunt of Mother-in-law's foul moods. Her mother-in-law's standards were very high. A tongue lashing in the kitchen if the ingredients were not prepared properly and lacked finesse, a smack on the hand if the *bunga kantan* or kaffir lime leaves were not cut finely enough, or the potato cubes were not of the same consistent shape. A yelling if the *sambal belachan* had no *oomph*. A nasty pinch if she found a speck of dust on the mother-of-pearl inlay furniture or grime on the Venetian mirrors.

"Hopeless! You women all *tak guna*!" Mother-in-law would grumble incessantly.

Although she had a battalion of servants, Mother-in-law herself liked to dust the furniture every morning, pottering around the halls with a feather duster. Lately, with each passing grand-childless year, she had taken to fastidiously dusting the imposing portraits of the family ancestors hanging in the front hall, muttering "*Sial, Sial*" under her breath, jabbing at the sepia photos with the brown and black chicken feathers.

Sue Kwan's husband retreated more and more into his world of business dealings and property acquisitions. A reticent man, he was content to immerse himself in his books and business ventures, leaving the running of the household to his mother, the matriarch of the clan. In the evenings, after a glass of sherry and dinner, he headed to the Malacca Gentlemen's Club. He seemed to be visiting it very frequently lately, coming home late at night, creeping clumsily into bed beside her. If she could only have a baby, maybe he would stay home more, Sue Kwan thought. Her stomach contracted in fear. What if Bebe changes her mind? A promise after all is just a verbal declaration, nothing legal.

Girl or boy? Sue Kwan pondered. Going by the laws of probability, it might just be a boy as Bebe already had three girls. But then, chromosomes never did subscribe to mathematics.

It turned out to be a boy.

Sue Kwan tried to look cheerful and celebratory when she attended the Mua Guek, the First Full Moon dinner of Bebe's baby boy, nursing dashed hopes and heartbreaking disappointment. She gave Bebe a tearful congratulatory hug. It was an extravagant occasion with much rejoicing over the baby boy, the first male of that generation of the Wee family. The family line was finally assured.

Guests were wined and dined at a sumptuous feast, presented on exquisite rose-pink porcelain, specially commissioned from the best kilns in China. Hard-boiled eggs, dyed red early that morning, were served with homemade pickled ginger. Nyonya *kueh* prepared by Ng Kim, the famous Bibik from Kandang, renowned for making such fabulous cakes you were reduced to whimpers of delight, were served in red and black lacquer baskets gilded in gold.

A famous Malaccan band, the Medallions, played waltzes, polkas, swing and *joget* numbers, while guests danced, regaled each other with *dondang sayang* verses, and celebrated the arrival of the male scion of a rich and powerful family.

In the midst of all the revelry, Sue Kwan managed to catch Bebe for a fleeting moment in a corner of the room.

"Bebe, please, next time, if it's a girl, please give her to me. Don't forget your promise."

"Next time? What next time? Oh no, no more babies for me. This is my fourth! That's quite enough. I'm sorry, Sue Kwan," Bebe replied firmly.

Two months later, Bebe was pregnant again.

It was a difficult pregnancy. Bebe was nauseous most of the time, unable to bear the smell of any kind of food. In the mornings and evenings, when the itinerant hawkers came around selling satay, *rojak* or *chee cheong fun*, calling out their wares, she would throw up, revolted at the thought of food.

In her final month, she found it hard to sleep with the weight of the baby pressing down on her. Early one morning, feeling hot and sticky, she decided to go downstairs rather than toss around in bed.

Softly she crept down the narrow spiral staircase to the third hall facing a lovely inner courtyard where a goldfish-shaped fountain trickled water into a large earthenware urn, embossed with dancing dragons. It was her favourite corner of the magnificent Peranakan house. She sat beside the marble table, enjoying the soothing tinkling sounds of the fountain, fanning herself languidly. The clammy humidity was oppressing.

Then, she heard a tap-tap tapping and a muffled sound from way back of the house. Who could it be at this unearthly hour? It was still dark, dawn hadn't arrived yet and all the servants were still asleep. Bebe walked through two more halls of the long narrow house into the kitchen. There it was again. Someone was knocking persistently on the back door. She wanted to summon the servants but decided it was too much bother. She would attend to it herself.

The back door was a heavy red wooden door, lashed securely with a horizontal wooden bar and four bolts. Bebe removed the bar, unlocked the bolts and tugged at the door. It would not budge. She tried heaving it open until she felt dizzy with exertion. One more pull, and then she almost fell back when it suddenly came open.

Bebe strained to see what was out there. It was pitch black outside. Something materialised in front of her. A tall dark figure in flowing white stood just a few feet away from her. She tried to make out its face but all she could see were the whites of a pair of eyes and another eye on the forehead. The figure put out an arm towards Bebe. She screamed in terror then fainted. She felt her baby kicking just before she blacked out.

When Bebe opened her eyes, she saw the entire household had been awakened. A circle of faces hovered around her anxiously. Servant girls were fanning and fussing over her, her Amah was rubbing her ubiquitous Chinese medicated oil on her temples, Mother-in-law was ordering someone to fetch the Tiger Balm from her room.

Guan, her husband stepped into her gaze and asked in a worried tone, "Bebe, are you alright?"

"I saw s…sss..something," she stammered, distraught. "Something was out there. A ghost. *Hantu*."

Guan said calmly, "Bebe, it wasn't a *hantu*. It was the *chettiar*."

He added, displeased, "Apparently, some of the servants

have been borrowing money from him."

Bebe smiled weakly when Param the local moneylender stepped forward sheepishly, contrite at having caused such a commotion. Tall, wiry and extremely dark skinned, he greeted Bebe with a Namaste gesture. He was clothed in a white *dhoti*, the back part of which was pulled forward between his legs and tucked in at the front. When he talked, his white teeth glittered and the whites of his eyes shone in stark contrast to his gleaming black complexion. The white *pottu*, a round dot of powder on his forehead gave him the appearance of a third eye. With a lot of head shaking and gesticulating, he tried to explain.

"I am so very sorry, Madam. A thousand apologies. Your driver, Ah Soon, and your butler, Ah Hock, they borrowed money from me but they are taking a long time to be returning me. They are owing me helluva...er I mean...a bloody lot of money. I am coming here early this morning to collect my money because I am going outstation today. But those rascals were sleeping."

He slapped his forehead with his palm in exasperation. "Madam, whatever are you doing at the back side of the house? I am so sorry to be frightening you out of your wits, Madam. My humble apologies."

Bebe clutched her tummy uneasily. She could feel her baby kicking again.

"Ahhh, all's well then," she said, though feeling very unwell and signalled for her maids to help her back to her bedroom upstairs.

She could hear Guan offering to pay Param the money which the servants owed him, and Mother-in-law lecturing the servants on the horrors and pitfalls of gambling although she herself played a mean hand at *chiki*, her favourite card game.

When Bebe unexpectedly went into labour two weeks before the due date. Sue Kwan decided to drop in at Bebe's place. When she arrived at the Wee household, she was puzzled at the tight-lipped silence of the staff instead of celebration on the arrival of another baby. Sue Kwan rushed upstairs to Bebe's room, worried that something had gone wrong. The master bedroom door was closed. Sue Kwan knocked urgently on the door.

Bebe's husband, Guan, looking pale and grim, opened the door and let her in without a word.

Sue Kwan was astonished at the disarray inside. Bebe's mother-in-law, a dainty lady with silver hair and all of five feet tall, was in a flap, wailing into a big hanky which she wore tossed on her shoulder, screeching for her pot of Tiger Balm ointment. Bebe's mother, who had come to visit her daughter, also looked very upset, running to and fro trying to calm Bebe's mother-in-law who was sitting at one corner of the huge bedroom, sniffling into her embroidered handkerchief. Bebe was sitting up in her bed, sobbing and crying. The doctor and nurses stood by nervously, unsure of what to say or do, while the servants ran in and out of the room, trying to look busy but all eyes and ears taking in the scene for juicy gossip in the servants' quarters later.

Guan, pacing up and down the room, pulled himself to his fullest height, walked up to Bebe and said, "Alright, Bebe, tell me. Who is it?"

"What do you mean 'Who is it'? I am in pain and it's all your blinking fault, and you dare ask me whoizzit!" the usually serene Bebe screamed at Guan.

Bebe's mother strode up to Guan and barked, "What are you implying here, Son-in-Law? My daughter is a very good girl."

Mother-in-law meanwhile was moaning into her hanky, "What will people say? What will people say? *Aiyo, malu.*"

The bedroom door swung open suddenly and in waddled chubby Ah Sum puffing excitedly. She announced triumphantly, "I know who did it. It was the *chettiar*!"

Mother-in-law, startled out of her wits, started to incant, "Oh *chetti chetti, lu mau mati.*" She grabbed the little pot of Tiger Balm and dabbed copious amounts on her temples and nostrils.

Bebe's mother marched across the room to confront Ah Sum. "What are you talking about? Ah Sum, how can you say such a thing?" screeched both mother and daughter.

"*Hai-yah*, I mean Bebe got *chiung*. She got shock by *chettiar* this morning. She got *chiung-lah*...baby come out same colour like *chettiar*! *Aiyah*, Ah-Tai Soh, why you open the door in the middle of the night? Why you no call me?

Got so many servants, for what? Now how-*ah* baby black in colour?"

For awhile everyone was stunned at this bizarre explanation. Yet, Ah Sum had a point there. The old nyonyas always nagged pregnant women to avoid any kind of unwelcome surprises, warning that if they were unlucky, the baby would take on the characteristics of the person or the object that frightened her.

Guan muttered, "What the heck is Ah Sum talking about? Is there such a thing?"

Bebe's mother interjected, "Ah Sum is correct. I think my daughter *kena chiung*. 'Spooked' as the English educated would put it. It has happened before. My sister was eight months pregnant, a real busybody *kaypoh*, cannot sit still for one minute. She tried to hammer a nail in the wall to hang up a picture or something. She accidentally hammered her finger. When her baby was born, he had a cleft lip."

"Ooowww, yes-oohh, I think Bebe *kena chiung*. My cousin sister in Taiping also got spooked. Gave birth to a boy hairy as a monkey. She was seven months pregnant, plucking rambutans in the backyard when a monkey pounced on her," Bebe's mother-in-law contributed her version in between spasms of sobbing.

Guan turned to the doctor.

"Doctor Loong, what do you say? What's your take on this?" Guan asked.

"*Ahem*...I'm afraid science sometimes can't explain everything, Mr Wee. Stranger things have happened for which medical science cannot provide any rational answers," explained the doctor.

Bebe threw herself back into the pile of pillows and started crying again.

Sue Kwan could not understand what they were talking about. Where was the baby? Her eyes searched the room frantically. At the far end near the window, she saw the midwife putting a little bundle swathed in white into a cradle. Sue Kwan tip-toed over, her heart in her mouth. When she peered into the cradle, she was stunned. The baby was very dark in complexion, the colour of lush ebony. The sunshine filtering in through the window, spotlighted the infant, making the baby's skin glisten.

The midwife whispered to Sue Kwan, squinting disapprovingly, "It's a girl. *Kesian dia*. Poor thing. So black, how to find husband next time."

The baby was asleep, her long eyelashes sweeping her cheeks. She had lovely delicate features and a tiny rosebud mouth. Sue Kwan stared at her in stupefied wonder. A girl...it was a girl. The baby opened her eyes and stared back at Sue Kwan. She gurgled and smiled. Sue Kwan picked up the infant in her arms and walked over to Bebe.

"It's a girl, Bebe. You have a girl!"

"I know," Bebe answered.

Sue Kwan in a tremulous voice, piped up again, "Bebe, do you remember your promise? You promised if it is a girl, you would give her to me."

"You don't have to feel obligated. If you don't want her,

I won't hold you to the promise," responded Bebe flatly.

"Don't want her? I want her more than anything in the world," said Sue Kwan.

"Then she is yours, Sue Kwan. She's yours."

The little baby, with the twinkling eyes and glistening skin, cooed and laughed, looking from one mother to the other.

Kalu jodoh tak mana lari
(If fated, there's nowhere to run.
Meaning: There is no running away from
one's love match.)

Rambut sama itam, ati orang mana sama
(We all have the same black hair
but no heart is the same.
Meaning: Who knows the heart of men?)

Baba idioms from
William Gwee Thian Hock, 1993.
Mas Sepuloh: Baba Conversational Gems
(Singapore Armour Publishing)

Jewellery was a nyonya's prized possession. Nyonyas love to adorn their hair, ears, neck, chest, fingers, arms and ankles with gold, silver, diamonds, jade, rubies and pearls. They will wear jewellery even when mourning; these are usually silver pieces inset with pearls which connote tears of sadness. (Clockwise from top) A set of kerosang serong *used to fasten the* baju panjang*;* intan *and gold earrings and ring; a pair of gold earrings.*

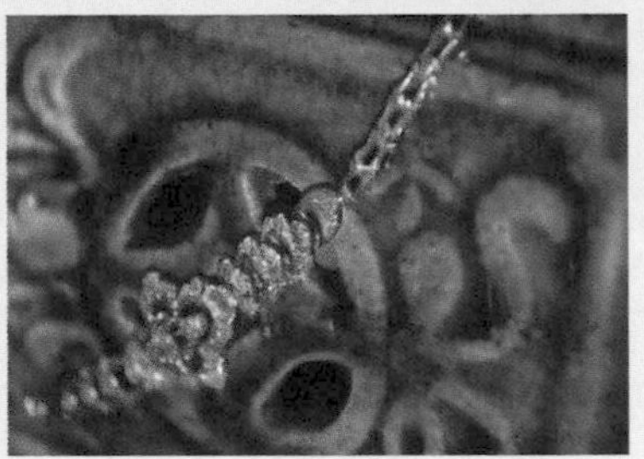

(Clockwise from top) A pair of gold earrings set with intan *or 'rose diamonds'; a diamond bracelet; a diamond pendant*

Son Boy and Sisters

I'm fed-up. Absolutely sick of friends teasing me about my name.

Son Boy. That's my name.

Sounds alright, you may think. I don't disagree. Only problem is – I'm a girl. It's not like my parents had run out of names when Mum became pregnant for the fourth time. All my three elder sisters have exquisite names. My eldest sister is named Ruby, my second sister Sapphire, my third Emerald.

Then Dad got fed up.

"I want a boy," he told my Mum assertively.

A friend had told him his girls' names were too beautiful and the spirits were jealous and would continue bestowing him with daughters. That's when he panicked.

When I was born, Mum was quite happy to be blessed with another girl. She already had a name in mind to top up her semi-precious stones series.

"Husband," she said, "Let's call her Diamond."

"No! No more of your fanciful names. Enough of rubies, sapphires, emeralds, and now diamonds. I already have a name for her. Son Boy."

"What? SON BOY?! Are you crazy? No daughter of mine is going to be called that ludicrous name."

"It's strategy. After Son Boy, we will definitely get a boy."

"Whatever happened to your biology lessons? Don't be absurd."

"Oh ho...you'll be surprised. Dr Tao, my feng shui master, told me we've got to break the chain."

"You're out of your mind. If you think I'm going to let you, you'd better think again!"

I was too young to know what transpired. Ruby told me much later there was a big fight. Dad got his way and I was named Son Boy. Mum wouldn't speak to Dad for weeks. But they must have connected again, because a year later, Mum got pregnant and this time it was a boy. Dad couldn't stop gloating for days.

He wanted to name his firstborn son after some famous Chinese hero or military officer but Mum insisted on Arthur as in King Arthur and the Knights of the Round Table.

"Bah, you and your English literature and your bloody English heroes. Why can't you be more Chinese? Why all these poncey English names? You Straits-born people are weird," grumbled Dad who was born into a Cantonese family in Gopeng and had a very Chinese upbringing and Mandarin-medium education.

"I didn't hear you complaining when you were courting me," snapped Mum. "Oh now I'm weird, is it? Back then, I was a dusky, exotic nyonya."

She added, "You're the one who's weird calling our daughter Son Boy! Don't blame me if she starts growing hair on her chest."

"Okay, okay, let's compromise then," Dad pleaded. Although my Pa was a very rich, successful and cunning, I'm told, businessman, he was quite wary of Mum's sharp tongue.

Finally, they agreed to settle on the full works. My little brother was named after both the English king as well as the Chinese general – Arthur Loh Sun Tse. We all preferred to call him Arthur.

During those growing up years, we were quite a close-knit family – Ruby, Sapphire, Emerald, Arthur and I, Son Boy.

The problems came on thick and fast when we reached young adulthood and my sisters started getting the attention of the opposite sex. All three of them are beautiful, I have to admit. With names like theirs, you do get a head start in life, I suppose. I, on the other hand, was quite plain with stubborn spiky hair and lousy skin.

Ruby has thick black hair with reddish tints cascading to her shoulders, red pouty lips and sultry eyes a man could drown in. She drove all her boyfriends crazy with desire, I'm quite sure of that. She was studying Economics at the University of London and was about to graduate and return to Malaysia when she called up one day to say she wasn't. She had fallen in love with an Irish man, a postgraduate student in Political Science whom she'd met at an Irish bar. They planned to get married soon and wanted Mum and Dad to give their blessings.

Mum, who grew up on a diet of Barbara Cartland, Barbara Bradford and Denise Robbins during her teens, cooed with excitement. "Oh, of course Ruby. How terribly romantic. Any chance he's a Marquis or a Lord?"

"Oh, for heaven's sake, Mum. He's Irish," Ruby replied.

It was Dad who objected, and so vehemently it took us all by surprise.

"What?! Marry a *kwei lo*? Are you crazy? No daughter of mine is going to marry a *kwei lo*!"

This started another big fight between Mum and Dad.

"What's wrong with a *kwei lo*? And stop calling white people devils, will you? It's embarrassing. You China-born types are still suffering from the Opium Wars siege mentality or what? Ruby says Malachy is a wonderful man."

"Ma-what? What's his name again?"

"Malachy O'Connor. Our future son-in-law. She loves him deeply."

"Ma...Ma...Ma foot, she does! I'm not going to have ginger-haired, freckled little *ang mo* kids with Chinese eyes running around this house. No, I absolutely forbid it."

"Oh grow up, Husband. No one's asking you for permission in the first place, only your blessings. It's the eighties. It's a different world today. We don't have any say, we can only be there for them if things go wrong."

"*Chapalang*! I worked so hard all my life and what do I get? Do I need this? My golf buddies and business associates will laugh at me and my *chapalang* grandchildren!"

"What's *chapalang*, Dad?" I butted in.

"*Chapalang* is what you'll get if you don't mind your own business. Butt out, Son, and concentrate on your maths homework."

"*Chapalang* is a Malaysian bigot's definition for the offspring of mixed marriages, Boy," Mum tried to educate me.

Dad wrote to Ruby and threatened he would disown her if she married her Irish boyfriend. He ordered her to return home to Kuala Lumpur as soon as she finished her last course where he would reward her with a brand new BMW, a cushy job as director in one of his companies and a Rolex watch. He would introduce her to his Chinese business tycoon friends, many of whom had eligible sons who would make good husbands and filial sons-in-law.

Ruby's reply was, "Thanks but no thanks." Ruby was quite the chip off the old block.

I cringed knowing full well the battle of wills ahead. Sure enough, Dad made life miserable for everyone at home, yelling and snarling and kicking our poor mongrel, Putih, more often than usual. After downing three glasses of Laphroaig Single Malt Scotch with tiny amounts of water one evening, he called his lawyer and announced loudly for all to hear.

"Mr Gucharan Singh, I want you to change my will. Strike out my eldest daughter's name. No share of my property for her, you hear me?" he growled, then told Mum to inform Ruby.

That didn't seem to bother Ruby one bit. She and her sweetheart, Malachy, flew to his hometown, Limerick in Ireland, a fortnight later and got hitched.

The wedding photos arrived soon after — Ruby looking radiant in a white *cheongsam* with a posy of white roses, daisies and babies' breath on her hair, and handsome, flaming red-haired Malachy in a tartan kilt in a charming garden setting. Mum showed the photos proudly around to her relatives who ooh-ed and aah-ed over them, while Dad sat black-faced, arms folded across his chest, scowling.

All was relatively quiet for some time. No one dared bring up the topic of Ruby's marriage for a while till things cooled down. Then one night, we were halfway through dinner when the phone rang. It was a call from my second sister Sapphire, studying law at the University of Kent.

Sapphire was attractive in a cool, elegant and classy way, and clearly the smartest of us all. She was very well-read, a real intellectual type and extremely articulate. I couldn't understand half the bombastic words she used. She could out-talk anyone. During her school days, she was the star of her school debating team. Consistently on the Dean's list at university, she was a formidable scholar with beauty and brains. Dad had big plans for her to work for his company and sue anyone who dared cross him.

Mum answered the call in the second hall and was on the line for quite a long time. Meanwhile, Dad was enjoying his dinner of stir-fried veggies with gingko nuts and steamed white pomfret in soy sauce with mushrooms.

He was in a relatively calm mood as his wife had finally complied with his wishes after his incessant grumbling and cooked him a 'proper Chinese meal'. He had had enough of her Nyonya curries and raging hot *sambal* dishes. I loved Mum's wonderful Peranakan dishes but Dad complained they were too 'heaty' and gave him indigestion.

Mum came into the kitchen with an inscrutable expression and said, "That was Sapphire. I have good news and bad news, Husband. The bad news is she has broken up with her childhood sweetheart, Lum Ah Kow."

Dad rejoiced, "Hey, ha ha, that's not bad news, that's good news! Never could stand that pimply mousy young man. And what a name. Imagine our Sapphire being called Mrs Lum Ah Kow!"

"And what's the good news?" asked Dad when Mum kept quiet.

"The good news is she has found someone else. A South African journalist she met at a civil rights demonstration in London last month."

Dad spluttered on his double boiled chicken soup with winter melon.

"A what? A...Aff...a...African? You call that good news? That's **** bad news!"

"I didn't say African. I said, South African."

"I don't care if it's north, south, east or west! He's African. Has she gone mad? What's wrong with Asian men? Why African? What are my daughters trying to do to me? *Chee sin...Fatt sun keng...Chan hai ow huit lor!*"

Dad started swearing and could hardly swallow another mouthful.

"You sent your girls abroad to widen their horizons, didn't you? It's to their credit they are not colour fixated like you!" Mum barked at Dad. "And stop swearing in Cantonese, will you? So crude!"

"I sent them to get an education. The all-important paper qualifications! I didn't ask them to bring back the United Nations!" Dad shouted.

"Er...are South Africans black or white, Dad? Huh... Mum?" I queried.

"Shaddup, Son! Eat your Chinese mushrooms," Dad yelled.

Dad tried to persuade Sapphire to dump her African sweetheart and return home ASAP with promises of a fully-paid deluxe condominium in Mont Kiara, a Mercedes S-class series, a country club membership and two Rolex watches. She didn't even have to work for the first year if she didn't want to.

Sapphire sent home her response in a long letter to Dad using such complicated, polysyllabic words even Dad and Mum gave up trying to understand her theories on the meter...er meta...metaphysics of physical attraction and the divee...er...divinity of love, juxtaposed with the transit... er...transient nature of material wealth. She also enclosed a photocopied article entitled something or other on bondage, about petty...er...petra... patriarchy and the female condition. Dad could not fathom a word of it.

"Look! Look at all my thousands of hard-earned dollars and what it has done to her brain. Gone cuckoo!" Dad complained.

"Why are you freaking out? She's just dating him. They haven't even talked of marriage yet," Mum retorted.

"Well, she'd better watch out or else...or else I'll call my lawyer Mr Gucharan Singh again," he threatened.

"You know Sapphire. She thrives on ideas and ideology. Your money doesn't matter a jot to her."

"It's all your fault," he scolded Mum. "You and your stupid, arty-farty notions of love you've been feeding our daughters with!"

"Well, excuse me, they sure are a lot cleverer than me in their choices."

"Ouch," I muttered quietly, just in case I got told to shaddup again.

All eyes were on Emerald now. Arthur and I were still too young to get entangled in this girl-boy business. I didn't even dare tell anyone I was having a crush on a senior school prefect in my all-girls' school — tawny tanned Rozita, ace discus and javelin athlete and long distance runner.

Emerald was Dad's favourite and I was quite sure she

would deliver. Deliver what I don't know but no, no way she would go against Dad's wishes, I was sure of that.

Dad wasn't that sure, I think, because he refused to send her to the United Kingdom for further studies. Instead, he sent her to the National University of Singapore. Plenty of 'normal' bachelors there, I heard him pronounce triumphantly while Mum rolled her eyes in disgust.

Emerald did not protest unfairness. She was a sweet, gentle girl, always laughing, very *manja*, the touchy feely type who loved soft toys and Mozart and cried over sad movies. Sentimental like Mum, she was quite happy to be near home and did not like to stray too far from her comfort zone. She loved animals and wanted to pursue a course in Veterinary Science but Dad told her there was no future in taking care of animals in this country and she was persuaded to switch to Biochemistry instead.

After her first year at university, I sensed something was wrong when she didn't call home anymore or come back for quick visits over long weekends. Then one day, a letter came in the mail from Emerald, addressed to Mum. I got to hear the contents when Dad came home from work.

Mum said, "I've news from Emerald. I won't do the good news-bad news routine this time, Husband. You figure it out."

"What? Does she need more money? I've already topped up her bank account in Singapore, plus given her another supplementary credit card."

"She doesn't want your money, she wants your

understanding."

"Understanding what?"

"She is in love with...well, at least, half a Chinese."

"What...what do you mean by half a Chinese? You're either Chinese or you're not. No halfway business. What the hell does that mean?"

"She's in love with a Chindian."

"What? What tribe is that? I didn't know there were tribes living in Singapore."

"Oh for goodness sake, he's half Chinese half Indian."

"A Chinese Indian? What on earth? How the heck can that happen?"

"Many things can happen, my dear, that are way beyond your limited comprehension."

"And what...what...is his Chinese name?" Dad demanded.

"He doesn't have a Chinese name. His mother is Chinese. His father is Indian, actually not Indian but Sri Lankan. His surname is Chandrasegaran."

"That makes him a Chinilankan or a Lankachi, Dad," I piped in helpfully.

Dad flopped down on his big chair and clutched at his chest.

"Oh-oh, er...Mum, do I call the doctor or the lawyer?"

"Shaddup, Boy," Mum said.

The nyonya sarong kebaya is not complete unless worn with jewellery, beaded shoes, silver belt and a silver or beaded bag.

Left: My mother, Foo Kwee Hoon (Beautiful Cloud) and to her right, her sister, Foo Kwee Guat (Beautiful Jade)

The Island

"No pork. Anybody here got bring pork? *Tolong buang*. Throw away. Or else I not going to the island. And you not going too," the boatman reminded us one more time before we boarded the boat for Pulau Besar.

"*Jangan main-main*," he warned, "the spirits on Pulau Besar are powerful."

My twin brothers were dancing about on the jetty, dressed in their spanking new branded outdoor gear, their baseball caps worn back to front. Their rhythmic jerky movements weren't exactly inspired by extreme excitement or anything like that; rather, it was because of the trance music from those thingies perpetually stuck in their ears.

"Hey, did you two hear what he said?" I snapped at them and tried to pull the ear plugs out of the twin standing next to me. He ducked and stuck out a reddish, sugar-coated tongue at me.

Mum scolded, "Cindy, leave them alone. Let them enjoy themselves."

The twins grinned irritatingly, and continued bobbing along with the throbbing din from their MP3 players, heads nodding, bodies twitching perpetually.

They were eleven years old, just five years younger than me, but we were so completely different. I love history, nature and books. They were the opposite – they never read at all, loathed history or anything older than ten days. They would start sweating within minutes if the air was not 'conditioned'. Their idea of a perfect day was chatting to cyberspace friends on their PCs and playing computer games till the cows come home.

When Dad told us about this trip, they responded with their usual 'enthusiasm' whenever it meant going into the outdoors.

"Awwww, must we? An island? Ewww, how boring," said Damien.

"How long does it take to get there? Where is it? What? In Malacca? You mean we have to go all the way to Malacca? Uggh, why can't we stay at home?" said Brendan.

"Oh quit complaining. You've never even been to an island before," I told them. "Come to think of it, you've never been anywhere remotely close to nature!"

Damien and Brendan immediately ganged up on me.

"Who sez so? I've been to the pyramids of Egypt and the ruins of Angkor," Damien the smart-aleck shot back.

"Yeah, I've shot savages from my jet plane! And bombed terrorists in the deserts!" Brendan retorted.

"In front of the PC without moving your lazy bums? Yeah, right," I scoffed.

"And by the way, pyramids are manmade, stupid," I added sarcastically. "Do you guys even know what nature means?"

"Nature? Nature means hot, sticky and sweaty. Yechh! Hey, Sis, are you sure you want to go to this island ? Think of the mozzies! No toilets...you will have to dig a hole or do it in the *lalang*...yucckk...think of the leeches coming for you. Ha ha ha!" Brendan teased me.

Damien whined, "An island, Dad? Awww, who needs to go to an island, Dad? I can just google it for you. It's like the real thing. Virtual island, no sweat. Save on petrol, Dad."

"Okay, that's enough. We are going. We will stay over at Aunty Bee Neo's place in Malacca town on Saturday night, then leave for Pulau Besar early the next morning. I've already confirmed with your aunt. She has booked us all a place on the boat trip to the island," Dad announced firmly, always happy to return to his hometown, Malacca.

The night before our trip, we had dinner with Aunty Bee Neo, Dad's sister, at the Portuguese settlement in Malacca. Aunty Bee Neo was a rambunctious jolly woman who loved to talk and couldn't stop once she started. She warned us to refrain from eating pork on the eve of our outing to Pulau Besar, and more importantly, not to bring anything containing pork along on our trip.

"Why all this strange *pantang-larang* about Pulau Besar?" Mum asked Aunty Bee Neo, as we tucked into a delicious spread of crabs smothered in a spicy-sweet sauce. "Surely they are just superstitions, right?"

"Well, it's better to play safe. Why ask for trouble? Pulau

Besar is a holy place. There are many graves there. They have been there for hundreds of years. The locals believe the spirits on the island have supernatural powers. Powerful *keramat* we must not offend.

"Last year, a boat going to Pulau Besar overturned in a storm and three passengers drowned. Maybe it was the storm or maybe someone offended the spirits. Who knows?

"Three years ago, something strange happened. One member from the group was a real show-off. Very destructive behaviour. He chased the tiny pink baby crabs scuttling around on the sand bars, and stomped on them, trying to kill them all.

"As if that wasn't enough, he yanked hermit crabs out of their shells. He and some of his friends thought the naked crabs looked absolutely hilarious. I thought he was quite sick in the head. Then, he did something very cruel. He skinned some frogs alive."

"Cool," piped the twins. I gave them a kick under the dinner table.

Aunty Bee Neo carried on, "He went too far. Some say they weren't actually frogs. Whatever it was, he offended the spirits of the island.

"After the trip, he fell very ill and almost died. He managed to pull himself back from the brink and that's because his mother went to seek help from the local *bomoh*. But he went blind in one eye. The doctors couldn't explain why. They didn't even know how to diagnose his illness. Now how do you explain that?"

In a serious tone, she added, "Whether you believe it or not, it's best to observe the local customs. Tomorrow, on our trip, don't harm or kill anything on the island. And remember, no pork allowed."

"You heard that, children?" Mum turned to us.

"Yeah, Mum," I mumbled, struggling to dislodge a sliver of crab shell from my teeth.

As for the twins, they were busy licking their gravy-laden fingers, while trying to send text messages from their mobile phones. I wasn't sure if they were even paying attention at all.

The next morning, Mum bought some packets of *nasi lemak* from the local market, and packed them into a picnic basket together with some fruits and drinks.

"There, that's safe enough," Mum said. "No pork here. I'm not taking any chances. *Nasi lemak* from the Malay lady in the market should be quite alright."

The sea was serene as our boat headed out for Pulau Besar on a bright sunny morning. Throughout the first part of the journey, the sea was very calm, silvery and shimmering in the morning sunshine. A breeze blew gently over the Straits of Malacca. The salty sea spray mixed with the scent of muddy mangrove swamps was a delightful change from the metallic, foul smells of Kuala Lumpur.

The twins were excited for a while as the boat pushed

off from the jetty. They clambered about, running up and down the deck to the passenger area below. Their excitement quickly waned. Soon, they were playing on their portable Playstations, mouths open in concentration, tongues sticking out, eyes fixated on the zombies crawling all over the bright tiny screens, their thumbs operating faster than their brains.

I couldn't resist snitching to Dad and Mum.

"They're at it again. Can't they do anything without electricity or batteries? Why bother to come along? Might as well stay at home."

Dad mumbled something. He got up from his seat wearily, went up to the boys and snatched their toys away from them. They howled in protest.

"You can play with your toys anytime. It's not often we go on a trip like this," Dad growled.

"Look, boys, look – flying fish!" Mum yelled excitedly as a barrage of startled silver fish shot out through the water in a graceful arching dive.

The twins went up to the deck of the boat, folded their arms and stared glumly at the sea. After about an hour, we could see the island in the hazy distance. Pulau Besar looked like a pregnant woman lying on her back. In silent repose, she lay invitingly, looking up at a bright cloudless sky. I clambered onto the deck to get a better view.

As the boat edged nearer, the sea gradually changed colour, growing darker and murkier. We were puzzled at this sudden change. The waves became choppy, jabbing at our boat, jerking it about. The sky, all lightness and brilliance in the morning, turned surly, black clouds appearing from nowhere. The sea changed swiftly into a nasty, livid blue mass of water.

We were still quite some distance away from the island. The mood of the sea was palpable – turning nastier and angrier by the minute. The sea began to heave in huge swells under our boat. With each gigantic wave, the boat kept drifting and veering broadside. It tossed about on the heaving choppy sea, its engines spluttering, reduced to a hapless piece of driftwood.

"Oh this is bad, this is really bad. Something terrible is going to happen," wailed Aunty Bee Neo.

An enormous wave came from nowhere and splashed onto the deck, leaving us spluttering in stunned surprise.

The boatman started shouting angrily, "*Siapa bawa babi? Sudah kata jangan!* Who bring pork? I awredi say no, no, CANNOT! Now you see-*lah*, big problem!"

The rising hysteria in his voice frightened us.

Out on the horizon, violent streaks of lightning lit up the dark sky, creating crazy electrical patterns. An ominous cloud of rain dousing half of the landscape on the horizon was bearing down upon us. Within minutes, it reached us and bucketed down furiously. A screeching wind tore out from the direction of the island and lashed the sea into a churning frothy mass. It screamed all around us, tearing at our hair, our clothes. I had never encountered nature in such maniacal fury.

I saw Damien and Brendan clinging to each other, their eyes wide agog in disbelief. They could not believe the real world could be this spectacular, I was sure of it. If I hadn't been so frightened myself, I would have yelled, "Hey, betcha can't find a computer game to match this!"

Another wave washed onto the boat, soaking us all to the skin. Everyone on board screamed.

My parents yelled at the twins to hold on tight to their seats. A number of passengers started praying aloud. The boatman had turned quite pale and began ranting again, "*Siapa bawa babi? Buang, tolong buang!*"

Aunty Bee Neo took over.

"Did you hear what he said? Everybody, throw out anything you think has pork in it. For God's sake, hurry. Someone here has angered the spirits of the island and we will all surely pay for it."

Some of the passengers on the boat were so petrified they started tossing whatever belongings and food they had brought along into the sea.

"We are going to die..." sobbed a woman passenger.

Suddenly I saw the twins make a dash for their knapsacks that were tossed in a pile on the floor of the deck. They dug desperately around in their knapsacks. Out came their mobile phones, MP3 players, headphones. Finally, Brendan pulled out a lump of something wrapped in kitchen towel paper. Wobbling precariously as the boat heaved and bucked on the waves, he tottered to the edge of the boat, followed closely by Damien.

"Damien, Brendan," Mother gasped. "Get back inside here!"

The winds screeched and lashed at the boys. Brendan, with one hand holding on tight to Damien, drew himself upright and hurled the odd package into the sea, as another gigantic wave smashed onto the boat and tried to pull him under.

Dad and I ran onto the deck, grabbed the boys and dragged them back into the safety of the passenger area of the boat.

Then strangely, the storm gradually abated. The wind died down slowly from a howling roar. The black clouds dispersed and the sky became light again. Flashes of lightning still lit up the horizon occasionally. The deafening rumbles of thunder stopped. We couldn't believe our eyes. The dark raging sea changed from blackish-blue to light green dancing colours, white foam cresting its waves. The huge swells diminished slowly in size and intensity, the sea became calm and lost its dark, menacing mood.

I was still trembling with fear at our close call.

"You idiots! You nearly got us killed. What were you hiding in your knapsacks?" I screamed at the twins, half-crying with relief.

"*Apa lu bawak, huh? Celaka, budak ta' dengeh.* I cannot swim. Want me to drown? Didn't I tell you a hundred times – no pork? What did you throw out just now?" Aunty Bee Neo yelled in a rage, her plump figure still shaking like jelly.

"Tell the truth, boys. We saw you throw something away," said Mum, queasy and greenish from sea sickness. Dad was speechless with fury. All eyes were on the twins as they stood there, petrified, wet and shivering.

Brendan's lower lip trembled for a minute, then his face puckered and he burst into a loud bawl, almost as sudden as the onset of the storm,

"It's all Damien's fault," sobbed Brendan. He pointed accusingly at Damien, "He made me go and buy it near the jetty when no one was looking."

"Buy what exactly, Damien?" asked Dad barely audible, gritting his teeth, trying to control himself.

Damien burst into an equally loud bawl as Brendan.

He blubbered, "*Waaahhhh...sob...blubber...sob.* How am I to know it's pork? The stoopid sign said 'American Hot Dog'!"

About the Author

Lee Su Kim is a Malaysian writer whose creative, literary and cultural activist endeavours and scholarly works have received considerable attention in Southeast Asia and internationally. Her light touches of humour, dry wit, sharp observations and fluid prose can be enjoyed in her three bestsellers – *Malaysian Flavours: Insights into Things Malaysian, Manglish: Malaysian English at its Wackiest and A Nyonya In Texas: Insights of a Straits Chinese Woman in the Lone Star State.*

Her first collection of short stories, *Kebaya Tales: Of Matriarchs, Maidens, Mistresses and Matchmakers*, is a bestseller and was awarded the national Popular-Star Readers' Choice Awards (Fiction) in 2011. This was followed by *Sarong Secrets: Of Love, Loss and Longing. Manek Mischiefs: Of Patriarchs, Playboys and Paramours* completes her much loved trilogy of short stories on the Peranakan Babas and Nyonyas.

In 2019, she co-authored a new and latest edition of *Manglish: Malaysian English at its Wackiest* with Stephen Hall. She also wrote more new stories for the 10th anniversary edition of *Kebaya Tales*.

She was born in Kuala Lumpur to a baba from Malacca and a nyonya from Penang. Educated at the Bukit Bintang Girls' School, Kuala Lumpur, Su Kim holds a Bachelor of

Arts in English, a Diploma and Masters in Education from the University of Malaya, Kuala Lumpur.

She lived in the US for four years and earned a Doctorate in Education from the University of Houston in 2001.Formerly Associate Professor at the School of Language Studies & Linguistics, Universiti Kebangsaan Malaysia, where she lectured and researched on language, culture and identity, she is now a writer, educator and cultural activist.

Active in heritage advocacy, Su Kim is the Founding President of the Peranakan Baba Nyonya Association of Kuala Lumpur & Selangor (PPBNKLS). As the President of the Protem committee (2005-2008) and then as the first President of PPBNKLS (2008-2014), she was involved in promoting the baba nyonya culture and heritage and in forging links with the various Peranakan associations in the region.

She is also a public speaker and has given many talks, readings and presentations all over the world. An invited speaker at the Ubud Writers and Readers Festival and the Singapore Writer's Festival, she has a Youtube video sharing her love for writing and her unique heritage – "A Nyonya Journey" at TEDx Petaling Street 2017.

Also by the author:

- *Sarong Secrets: Of Love, Loss and Longing*
- *Manek Mischiefs: Of Patriarchs, Playboys and Paramours*
- *Manglish: Malaysian English at its Wackiest*
- *Malaysian Flavours: Insights into Things Malaysian*
- *A Nyonya In Texas: Insights of a Straits Chinese Woman in the Lone Star State*

Visit www.leesukim.com and follow Su Kim on Facebook at: www.facebook.com/Lee-Su-Kim/Author